The animals must be killed—quickly—before the patrollers are called."

Troy was startled. Certainly he had no intention of yielding to that. "Why?" he asked.

Zul's eyes changed. "If you do not know, then you know nothing. They are a danger—to all of us, now that their master is dead. You will kill them, or you will wish that you had died also."

Troy caught Zul by the collar, pulled him to his feet. "You will tell me why these animals are a danger," he said.

"Because they think, they take orders, they report . . . *they are more than animals. . . ."*

"Once more Andre Norton whirls her reader far into space worlds of the future and adventures in interplanetary intrique . . . fast-moving . . . sure to absorb science-fiction fans."

—*Kirkus Reviews*

Fawcett Crest Books
by Andre Norton:

CATSEYE

Andre Norton

FAWCETT CREST • NEW YORK

CATSEYE

THIS BOOK CONTAINS THE COMPLETE TEXT OF THE
ORIGINAL HARDCOVER EDITION.

Published by Fawcett Crest Books, a unit of CBS Pub-
lications, the Consumer Publishing Division of CBS Inc.,
by arrangement with Harcourt Brace Jovanovich, Inc.

ISBN: 0-449-24285-4

Printed in the United States of America

First Fawcett Crest Printing: April 1980

10 9 8 7 6 5 4 3 2 1

One

Tikil was really three cities loosely bound together, two properly recognized on the maps of Korwar's northern continent, the third a sore—rather than a scar—of war, still unhealed. To the north and west Tikil was an exotic bloom on a planet that had harbored wealth almost from the year of its first settlement. To the east, fronting on the spaceport, was the part of Tikil in which lay the warehouses, shops, and establishments of the thousands of businesses necessary for the smooth running of a pleasure city, this exotic bloom where three-quarters of the elite of a galactic sector gathered to indulge their whims and play.

To the south was the Dipple, a collection of utilitarian, stark, unattractive housing. To live there was a badge of inferiority. A man from the Dipple had three choices for a cloudy future. He could try to exist without subcitizenship and a work permit, haunting the Casual Labor Center to compete with too many of his fellows for the very limited crumbs of employment; he could somehow raise the stiff entrance fee and buy his way into the strictly illegal but flourishing and perilous Thieves' Guild; or he could sign on as contract labor and be shipped off world in deep freeze with no beforehand knowledge of his destination or work.

The War of the Two Sectors had been fought to a

stalemate five years ago. Afterwards, the two leading powers had shared out the spoils—"spheres of influence." Several major and once richer planets had to be written off entirely, since worlds reduced to cinders on which no human being dared land were not attractive property. But a fringe of frontier worlds had passed into the grasp of one or the other of the major powers—the Confederation or the Council. As a result, the citizens of several small nations suddenly found themselves homeless.

At the outbreak of the war ten years earlier, there had been forced evacuations from such frontier worlds; pioneers had been removed from their lands so that military outposts and masked solar batteries could be placed in their stead. In this fashion, the Dipple had been set up on Korwar, far back from the fighting line. During the first fervor of patriotism the Dipple dwellers met with good will. But later, when their home worlds were ruined or traded away across the conference tables, there was resentment, and on some planets there were organized moves to get rid of these rootless inhabitants.

Now, before dawn in Tikil, men from the Dipple leaned their bowed shoulders against the outer wall of the Casual Labor Center or squatted on their heels before the door that marked the meeting place between the haves and the havenots.

Troy Horan watched the pale gold in the morning sky deepen. Too late to mark stars now. He tried to remember the sky over Norden—and had again one of those sharp picture flashes of recollection.

A silver bowl arching above a waving plain of grass, grass that was pale green, mauve, and silver all at once, changing as the wind rippled it. He knew the warmth of a sun always half veiled in rainbow haze, felt the play of muscles as the animal he perched upon as a small boy, rather than bestrode, broke into a rocking canter. That was one of his last memories of Norden. They had been out "riding track," cutting a wide circle about the grazing herd of tupan to check that none of the animals had drifted toward the quicksands near the river.

It had been that same morning that the Council ships had cut out of the sky, burning portions of the plain to charred earth and slag with their tailbursts. Within three days Troy and his people had left Norden for Korwar—three Horans, a small clan among all the others. But not three for long. His father—big body, laughing voice, quiet steady eyes, a pair of hands that did everything well, a man who was able to establish a strange bond of sympathy with any animal—had put on a trooper's tunic and vanished into the maw of a transport. Lang Horan had not returned.

After that the Big Cough had hit the Dipple, leaving only Troy Horan, a lanky adolescent who inherited skills/and desires for which there was no need on Korwar. He also possessed a stubborn, almost fierce independence, which had so far kept him either from signing on as contract labor or from the temptation offered by the Guild. Troy Horan was a loner; he did not take orders well. And since his mother's death, he had no close attachments in the Dipple. There were few left there now who had come from Norden. The men had volunteered as troopers, and, for some reason, their families had been particularly susceptible to the Cough.

The door that was their gate to the day's future slid

7

back. Men stood away from the wall, got up. Mechanically Troy made a brushing gesture down the length of his thin torso, though nothing would restore a vestige of trimness to his clothing.

Spacer's breeches, fifth-hand, clean enough but with their sky blue now a neutral, dusty gray; spacer's boots, a little wide for his narrow feet, the magnetic insets clicking as he walked; an upper tunic that was hardly more than a sleeveless jerkin, all in contrast to the single piece of his old life that he wore pulled tight about his flat middle. That wide belt of a Norden rider was well oiled, every one of its silver studs polished and free of tarnish. Those studs formed a design that was Troy's only heritage. If he ever rode the grass plains again, with tupan galloping ahead—well, those tupan might bear that same pattern on their cream-white hides. Lang Horan had been Range Master and Brand Owner.

Because he was young, tough, and stubborn, Troy was well to the fore of the line at the mechanical assigner. He watched with alert jealousy as three men ahead ran toward the stamper, assured of work—the mark on their wrists giving them the freedom of the city, if only for a day. Then he was facing that featureless, impersonal mike himself.

"Horan, class two, Norden, lawful work—" The same old formula he uttered there day after day. He stood, his feet a little apart, balancing as if the machine were an opponent ready for battle. Under his breath he counted five quickly, and a tiny hope was born. Since he had not been rejected at once, the assigner *did* have some request that might be matched by his meager qualifications.

8

The five he had counted doubled into ten before the assigner asked a question: "Knowledge of animals?"

"That of a Norden herd rider—" Troy stretched the truth to a very thin band, but his small hope was growing fast.

The assigner meditated. Troy, through his excitement, felt the impatience of the men behind him. Yet the length of time the machine was taking was so promising—

"Employed." Troy gave a small gasp of relief. "Time of employment—indefinite. Employer—Kossi Kyger, first level, Sixth Square. Report there at once."

The plates in his boot soles beat a rataplan as he hurried to the stamper, thrust his hand into the slot, and felt that instant of heat that set the work mark on his tanned wrist.

"First level, Sixth Square," he repeated aloud, not because it was so necessary to impress his memory, but for the pure pleasure of being able to claim a work address.

Sixth Square lay on the outer fringe of the business district, which meant that Kyger was engaged in one of the upper-bracket luxury trades. Rather surprising that such a merchant would have need for a C.L.C. hireling. The maintenance force and highly trained salesmen of those shops were usually of the full-citizen class. And why animals? Horan swung on one of the fast-moving roll walks, his temporarily tattooed wrist held in plain sight across his wide belt to prevent questions from any patroller.

Because it was early, the roll walks were not crowded, and few private flitters held the air lanes overhead. Most of the shutters were still in place across the

9

display fronts of the shops. It would be midday before the tourists from the pleasure hotels and the shoppers from the villas would move into town. On Korwar, shopping was a fashionable form of amusement, and the treasures of half the galaxy were pouring into Tikil, the result of stepped-up production after the war.

Troy changed to another roll walk. The farther westward he went, the more conspicuous he became. Not that clothing was standardized here, but the material, no matter how fantastically cut and pieced together, was always rich. And the elaborate hair arrangements of the men who shared the roller with Troy, their jeweled wristbands, neck chains, and citizens' belt knives, took on a uniformity in which his own close-cropped yellow hair, his weaponless belt, his too-thin, fine-boned face were very noticeable. Twice a patroller stirred at a check point and then relaxed again at the sight of the stamp on the boy's bony wrist.

Sixth Square was one of the areas of carefully tended vegetation intended by the city planners to break the structure pattern of the district. Troy jumped from the roller and went to the map on a side pillar.

"Kyger," he said into the mike.

"Kyger's," the finder announced. "Gentle Homos, Gentle Fems—visit Kyger's, where the living treasures of a thousand worlds are paraded before you! See and hear the Lumian talking fish, the dofuld, the priceless Phaxian change-coat—the only one of its kind known to be in captivity alive. Follow the light, Gentle Homo, Gentle Fem, to Kyger's—merchant dealer in extraordinary pets!"

A small spark, which had glowed into life on the wall below the map, loosed itself and now danced through the air ahead, blinking with a gem flash. A pet shop! The inquiry about animal knowledge was now explained. But Troy lost some of his zest. The thin story he had told the assigner was now thinner, to the point of being full of holes. He was ten years out of Norden, ten years away from any contact with animals at all. Yet Troy clung to one hope. The assigner had sent him, and the machine was supposed to be always right in its selection.

He looked about him. The massed foliage of the center square was a riot of luxuriant vegetation, which combined plants and shrubs from half-a-dozen worlds into a pattern of growing—red-green, yellow-green, blue-green, silver— And he began to long with every fiber of his semistarved body that he would be the one Kyger wanted, even for just one day.

His spark guide danced up and down, as if to center his attention on the doorway before which it had paused, and then snuffed out. Troy faced Kyger's display and drew a deep breath of wonder, for he seemed to be staring at four different landscapes, each occupying one-quarter of the space. And each landscape was skillfully contrived so that a section of an outlandish planet had been transported in miniature. In each, small creatures moved about the business of living and dying. It was all art tri-dee, of course, but the workmanship was superb and would completely enthrall any prospective customer.

Reluctantly Troy approached the door itself, a barrier where plexaglass had been impressed with a startling and vivid pattern of weird and colorful insects, none of

11

which he recognized. There was no sign that the establishment was open for business, and he had no guide to lead him behind the mass of buildings to a rear entrance. Troy hesitated uncertainly before the closed door until, among the imprisoned creatures of the center panel, a portion of face with reasonable human features appeared. Round dark eyes set in yellow skin regarded him with no trace of interest or emotion.

Troy held up his wrist so that the employment mark might be fully visible to those eyes. Unblinkingly they centered upon it. Then the stretch of yellow cheek, the broad nose, vanished. The creatures in the panel seemed to flutter as that barrier arose. And a flow of warm air, redolent with many strange smells, engulfed Troy. As if drawn by an invisible cord, he entered Kyger's.

He was given no time to look about the outer reception lounge with its wall cabinets of more miniature other-world scenes, for the owner of the eyes was awaiting him impatiently. Used as he was to oddities, human, humanoid, and nonhuman, Troy still found the small man strange enough to study covertly. He could have walked under Horan's out-stretched arm but his small, wiry body was well proportioned and not that of a dwarf. What hair he had was black and grew in small tufted knobs tight to the rounded bowl of the skull. In addition, there was a rough brush of the same black on his upper lip and two tufts or knots on his chin, one just below the center of his lower lip and the other on the point of the jaw beneath.

His clothing was the conventional one-piece suit of an employed subcitizen, with the striking addition of

12

a pair of boots clinging tightly to his thin legs and extending knee-high, fashioned of reptile skin as soft as glove leather, giving off tiny prismatic sparks with every movement of their wearer. About a slight potbelly he had a belt of the same hide, and the knife that swung from it was not only longer but also wider than those usually worn in Tikil.

"Come—" His voice was guttural. A crook of finger pointed the way, and Troy followed him through two more showrooms into a passage from which opened a number of screened doors. Now the effluvium of animal—a great many animals—was strong, and sounds from each of the screened doors they passed testified to the stock Kyger kept on hand. Troy's guide continued to the end of the hall, set his small hand into the larger impression of a palm lock, and then stood aside for Horan to enter.

If the yellow man was an oddity, the man who sat waiting for Troy to cross his office was almost as great a surprise. Horan had seen many of the merchants of Tikil, and all of them had been glittering objects indeed. Their jewels, their ultrafashionable dress, their eye-catching coiffures had all been designed as advertisements to attract general attention.

But Kyger, if this was Kyger, was no such starburst. His muscular body was covered with a hora-silk half tunic and kilt, but the color was a dark and sober blue, and he wore no jewels at all. On his right wrist was the broad service bracelet of a veteran spacer with at least two constellations starring its sweep, while his skull was completely shaven as if to accommodate the helmet of a scout-ship man. The bareness of that deeply tanned stretch of skin made the red,

13

puckered scar down along his right ear the more noticeable. Troy wondered fleetingly why he chose to keep that disfiguring brand; plastic surgery could have erased it completely.

The other regarded Troy for a long moment, his stare both as aloof and as searching as that the yellow man had used through the door panel.

"The assigner reported you as Norden," he remarked, but gave the planet name a slight accent new to Troy. "I would rather have thought Midgard—"

Troy met him eye to eye. This man had a spacer's knowledge of racial types and other worlds right enough.

"I was born on Norden—"

The other might not have heard him. "Midgard—or even Terra—"

Troy flushed. "Norden," he repeated firmly. Lang Horan's father had been from Midgard, right enough. Before that—well, who traced any planet-pioneering family back through generations and star systems to the first hop?

"Norden. And you think that you know something about animals." Those gray eyes, cold as space between far-flung suns, dropped from Troy's face to the belt with its lovingly polished silver studs. "Range Master, eh?"

Troy refused to be drawn. He shrugged, not knowing why the other was trying to bait him. Everyone knew that Norden had been handed over to the Confederation, that none of her former inhabitants could hope to return to her plains.

"All right. If the assigner sent you, you're the best it could find." Kyger arose from the enveloping embrace
14

of his eazi-rest. The yellow man slipped to his side. "Zul will give you your orders. We are expecting a shipment in on the Chasgar. You'll go to the dock with Zul and do just as he tells you—no more, certainly no less. Understand?" There was a flick of razor-sharp whip in that. Troy nodded.

Zul was certainly not a talkative companion. He merely beckoned Troy out through another door into a courtyard. This, too, was sided with pens and cages, but Troy was given no time to inspect their inhabitants. Zul waved him to a waiting flitter. As Troy took his place in the foreseat, the small man reached for the controls and they lifted with practiced ease to the air lanes. Zul circled, then headed them toward the west and the spaceport.

There was more traffic aloft now, personal flitters, heavier vans, and small flyers such as their own. Zul slipped through the lanes with a maximum of speed and a minimum of effort, bringing them down without a jar on the landing strip behind the receiver station. Again a jerk of thumb served to bring Troy, trailing his guide, into one of the many entrances of the clearance section. His small companion was well known here, for he bypassed two barriers without explanation, their guardians waving him on.

"Kyger's." Zul spoke at last, putting a claim disk down before the man in charge of the third grill.

"Right section, third block—"

Now they were in a corridor with a wall on one side, a series of bins, room size, on the other, each well filled with shipping crates, bales, and containers. There were men hauling these in and out, which testified that the contents of the packages in this particular section were too precious to be left to the mechanical transportation of the port robots.

Zul located the proper bin room and dropped his disk into the release frame at the door. The protecting mesh rolled up, and a light flashed on above two crates and a large, well-padded travel cage. All three packages were bulky, and Zul, fists on hips, eyed them closely before he said over his shoulder, "Get a truck."

Troy went back up the corridor to claim one of the motored platforms. He was wriggling that out of a line of its fellows when he caught a half glimpse of a face, a familiar face. As he jumped on the platform, dug his boot toe into the activating button, and headed the vehicle down the line, he wondered just what would happen if he shouted out that a newly accepted member of the Thieves' Guild was working here, in the very center of the supposedly best-protected treasure-transhipping center on Korwar. Every man who entered this building had been scanned by the psychocheck at the door, and everyone not on legitimate business would have been unmasked by that latest weapon in the armory of the patrollers. Yet Troy was certain he had seen Julnuk Varms shifting a crate, and he knew for a fact that Varms had crossed the line into the apprenticeship ranks of the Guild.

The platform rolled to a stop before Zul, and they went to work shifting their cargo to its surface. Each piece was heavy enough to require the combined efforts of the mismatched workers, and Troy wiped his hand across his face as the second settled into place. He eyed the curtains covering the sides of the cage, wondering just what kind of exotic creature cowered within.

16

Cowered? That was the wrong word. The inmate of that cage was curious, interested, alertly eager—not in any way cowed. Inmate? Inmates—two of them—

Troy stood very still, staring at the closely curtained transport cage. How did he know that?

Interest—now increasing— Something touched him, not physically, but as if a very soft, inquiring paw had been drawn lightly along his arm to test the quality of his skin, the strength of his muscles, the toughness of the bone beneath that covering. Just so did he feel that something had very lightly touched what was his inner self in exploration. Touched—and flashed instantly away—so that the sensation was cut off almost the same moment that he was aware of it. Troy helped Zul boost the cage onto the platform. There was no feeling of movement from within—nothing at all. Had there ever been?

Two

The cage was stowed with extra care just behind the driver's seat in the flitter, and during the transfer from warehouse to flyer there had been not the slightest sound from its interior. Yet twice more Troy had been aware of those paw taps of exploration, touches that were gone the instant he was alert to them. He was thinking hard as he left Zul in the flitter and went to return the platform. The other had shown no signs of

17

surprise or interest in the cage. Did Zul find those subtle inquiries ordinary—or did he not feel them at all? What kind or species of animal traveled in that container?

Native life on a thousand worlds was now known to spacers, explorer scouts, pioneers. And Troy had heard tales told in the Dipple by men gathered from planets in a wide sector of the galaxy. Yet never before had there been any suggestion that a form of life existed that was able to contact men mentally. Mentally!

Troy paused. Mentally! So—that was it! He had put a name to that elusive touch. But—

He did not know that his eyes had narrowed, that his fingers were drumming a faint tattoo on his belt. This was something to consider by himself. Out of the far past an emotion other than surprise awoke, sent a warning through him. Look, listen, and keep one's thoughts to oneself—the law of survival.

Troy swung around so suddenly that he caught the slight movement of a man he must have startled into that tiny betrayal. Varms stood just outside, his elbow resting on a pile of boxes, obviously waiting for orders. Yet he had been watching Troy, just as he was so patently not watching him now. Did Varms expect Horan to spark a patroller? He knew the inner laws of the Dipple better than that. As long as Varms made no move toward looting Kyger's, where Troy's loyalty was temporarily pledged, Horan would not reveal any knowledge of him.

He walked past Varms without a sign, heading toward the flitter. It was only chance that dictated the next warning. A porter was wrangling with one of the bin attendants, and they now carried their quarrel to the section manager. Since the object of their dispute was large, they were hot-tonguing it, not in the inner office but outside in the corridor. A length of crystal mirror, bright and backed with red-gold, bore a disfiguring crack down its side.

That crack might distort a reflection, but it could not conceal it. And in that patch of mirror Troy caught a glimpse of a tailer—Varms! The interest a new recruit of the Guild might have in a C.L. from the Dipple was negligible, but in a cargo—that was a different matter. And Varms, clumsy and inept as he was, might well be after the contents of the cage—or of the two crates that accompanied it.

Troy came out into the brightness of the flitter park. There were rows of waiting vans, very few passenger flyers. A series of two-story patroller towers quartered the whole area. There must be spy rays throughout every lane here. No one had ever dared a highjacking job in this place. And he did not see how he and Zul could be tackled once they were in the air— If they had been on wheel lock, now—

But he discovered that surface travel was just what Zul was intending. The wheels were extended from the body flaps, and the little man edged the vehicle out on ground level.

"What's the idea?" Troy folded his long legs into the cramped quarters beside Zul. "Don't we lift back?"

For the first time those wide lips split in something approaching a grin.

"No, no lift back." The other mimicked his tone. "We carry those who must ride easy."

Not much of an explanation, Troy thought. If the occupants of the cage had managed to survive passage

19

in a space freighter, they certainly could take very easily a short air flight back to Sixth Square. He had something other to chew on also—that move by Varms. Taken together with this action of Zul's, it began to make sense. Could the yellow man and the novice thief have rigged a highjack between them, with himself set up to pin the blame upon?

Troy dismissed that thought. Too many loose ends. He was not driving; Zul was. He could prove that he had had no connection with Kyger's before this morning, knew nothing of any cargo that was coming in for the shop. And somehow he was certain Zul was not planning any double cross of his employer—in spite of Varms. But there had to be a reason, other than the one he had been given, for this ground-level progress.

It was not a straight-line progress either, he noted. Troy knew the warehouse section of Tikil well enough to be certain with every block they passed that Zul was taking a round-about way. Why? A sidelong glance at the other's closed face argued that this was another question Zul was not going to answer.

Troy settled back as far as he could in a seat adjusted to Zul's comfort, not his own, and waited for further enlightenment. Once more he was conscious of activity in the cage, mental activity. It was no longer directed toward him, but at their surroundings. Troy's breath caught in a tiny gasp as he realized—picking impressions and hints out of those vague, strange currents—that the occupants of the cage were engrossed in studying their new surroundings. Yet how could they see through the thickly padded covering of the cage—unless that covering was not what it seemed to superficial examination?

20

He would have given a great deal at that moment to be able to turn and sweep the covering to the floor of the flitter, to see the unseen. A great deal, but not today's employment. Troy was very sure that such a move on his part would see Zul's summoning of the nearest patroller, his own ignominious and disastrous return to the Dipple. Curiosity was not spur enough to risk that.

They made two more unnecessary turns. There were other flitters wheeling—usually private jobs delivering passengers to the buildings, so Zul's method of progress was in no way extraordinary. But Troy's attention went now to the visa-screen above the controls. He watched for Varms—was the other still trailing?

He could pick out no following flitter that seemed suspicious. But Troy would be the first to admit that he could not match skills with any of the Guild. For all he knew, every one of those flyers and the men and women in them could be part of some fantastic scheme to loot the one in which he was traveling. Should he warn Zul?

The latter was driving at a rate well within the safety regulations of ground level. A portion of vulnerable skin and muscles between Troy's shoulders began to itch as the feeling of expectancy built up inside him. And his growing distrust was shared by those in the cage. Their interest had changed to a desire to warn—or alert—

Troy opened his mouth to speak. A yowling wail burst from the cage, loud enough to drown out any spoken word. Zul's head jerked up. The yowl sank into silence but Troy caught the message—danger was coming, and fast. His hand shot out, fingers fumbling with the catch of the arms locker. But his thumb pressure could not unlock it.

Zul sent the flitter into a burst of speed, which tore them out of the mouth of an avenue into one of the circles of space surrounded by the first ring of shops. With an expert's skill the small man wove a devious pattern among the other flitters there. Troy, tense, kept his attention divided between the path ahead and the near misses Zul guided them through. There had been no further outburst from the cage. But he did not need the wave of expectation issuing from there to warn him of trouble yet to come.

They might have made it free and clear had not Zul miscalculated, or been outplayed, by inches. Troy was slammed against the arms locker, his raised arm protecting his head, as the flitter smashed into an ornamental standard, edged into that to avoid the forward ram of another flyer.

The shock of his impact must have sprung the lock on the arms compartment. As Troy pushed back from it, the panel gaped and he grabbed the butt of a stunner inside. The arm that had taken the shock of his weight was numb, hanging heavy from his shoulder, but the other was all right and his fingers curled hungrily about the weapon.

On Zul's left the door had burst open, spilling the little man into the street. He was already dragging himself up, blood pouring from a cut over one eye. When he tried to stand, he gave a grunt and reeled back against the flitter, apparently unable to rest his weight on his right ankle.

Troy sent his shoulder against the door on his own side, went out and down in a roll, the stunner in his
22

hand and ready. He was sure he was going to face some aggressor more dangerous than any indignant flitter owner Zul might have scraped. As he brought up against the twin of the pillar they had crashed, he saw Zul draw his knife and a man leap with the ease of a trained street fighter from between two parked flitters.

There were pedestrians, a crowd of them, gathering. But until they knew that this was not some private challenge-fight, none would call a patroller. By drawing his belt knife instead of trying for a stunner, Zul had labeled this a meeting-of-honor, unorthodox as its setting might be. And had not Troy been warned, he might have hesitated to come to the other's assistance.

His numbed arm bothered him, and he rested the barrel of the stunner on his knees to take aim against the attacker. Knife blades flashed in the sunlight. Zul, his back braced against the wrecked flitter, was seemingly cornered and on the defensive from the first.

Troy pressed the firing stud of his weapon, remembering the long-ago training by Lang: "Point your barrel as you would your finger, boy. Aim means more than speed."

There was the faint "pssst" from the stunner. The man fronting Zul wavered, slewed partly around, and staggered back, bringing up against one of the parked vehicles, shaking his head dazedly. But the small man he had attacked did not try to follow up the advantage. Troy tapped with his thumb, sending another charge into the stunner.

He was just in time, for again that ear-torturing wail sounded from the interior of the flitter, and the impact of warning reached him full blast. Instinctively he hurled himself to the right. A knife struck the pillar and clattered to the ground.

The man who had hurled it was holding back, but his companion came on, ready for another try, his eyes narrow and calculating. Troy aimed at the other's head, praying he would not be wearing a force screen. The determination of the attack, and the time and place it had been delivered, argued that the Guild men either were after some fabulous loot or had been hired at the high rate, which in turn suggested they would have top equipment.

But Troy never had a chance to discover if his fears were correct. A white coil materialized out of thin air only a foot or so above the head of the advancing knifeman. It whirled in a circle, throwing off, with almost dizzying speed, a web of white filaments that fell about the attacker, touching and then clinging to shoulders, arms, body, and, finally, legs. The man struggled against the enwebment fruitlessly. Within a matter of moments he was down, as well packaged as a spider's prey. And a second web had taken care of his companion.

Troy straightened up, dropped the stunner to the ground well out in view, not having any wish for the patrollers to start in on him. Leaving the weapon where it lay, he went to Zul.

Blood made a gory and devilish mask of the small man's face, and he clung to the swinging door of the wrecked flitter with one hand, as if he needed that support badly. As Troy came to him, the younger man was suddenly aware of the fact that the warnings that

24

had flowed from the cage were at an end; there was no contact with its inhabitants now.

The first patroller took charge. Troy answered questions with the strict truth concerning what he had seen—but he did not mention the unheard warnings. And Zul either could not or would not elaborate on that report. Somewhat to Troy's surprise, Kyger himself stepped out of the second patrol flitter. And his efficiency matched that of the law. Zul was sent off to have his hurts tended before Kyger examined the cage. When Troy helped him swing it out to the pavement, he was brisk.

"No harm done, officer," he informed the patroller. "Apparently it was just an attempted highjack—not that such a theft would have done them any good."

"Why not?" The patroller was a Swatzerkan, his green-tinged skin showing a faint lacing of scales across the backs of his hands as he held a small recorder to catch their answers.

"Because these animals cannot live long without their own imported food and trained care, officer. They are a special order—for the Gentle Fem San duk Var—"

The Swatzerkan did not exactly blink, but perhaps there was a shade more deference in his voice when he replied, "You have indeed been favored by fortune, Merchant, in that your shipment did not fall into the hands of these worms' castings." His eyes touched briefly on the bound, or webbed, prisoners. "It will be your wishing to take these precious creatures to your shop. But one fears that your flitter is beyond the power of rising—"

"An accommodation will serve."

"Ah—so. Mulat, an accommodation for the merchant!"

One of the other patrollers went to the com unit of the official flitter. And for the first time Kyger appeared to really notice Troy.

"You used that?" He nodded toward the stunner still lying by the knife-scored pillar.

"Yes."

"Good enough." Kyger crossed to retrieve the weapon and hand it to the Swatzerkan. "I witness my man used this in defense of my goods," he said, using the formal, responsibility-assuming phrase.

"It is so noted, Merchant."

Troy stared at Kyger. Such a move was made on the behalf of a full-time employee, a subcitizen, not for a day laborer out of the Dipple. Did Kyger mean—?

But this was no time to ask questions. An accommodation flitter set down on the clear oval beyond the pillars, and Troy helped Kyger move the cage and the two crates into it. There was still nothing from the transport box. One could almost imagine that he had dreamed that questing thought process. But Troy's curiosity pricked the more fiercely after the events of the past half hour.

Any pets offered to the wife of Var suk Sark would indeed be the most exotic as well as the most expensive obtainable. Suk Sark was of one of the Fifty Noble Families on Wolf Three. But the Gentle Fem San duk Var was not accepted in that lineage-conscious assemblage. Gossip was undoubtedly correct in ascribing the present residence of the Var household on Korwar to that fact. One could not buy one's way into the Fifty, no matter how limitless was the pile of credits one could dip into. But there were other circles one could

26

impress with one's importance—many such on Korwar.

Troy wondered how suk Sark enjoyed running his autocratic government of the Sweepers from so far away. The Sweepers in the galaxy as a whole were small fry, a collection of six minor solar systems, and they never ventured too far into the conflicts between the real lords of space. But sometimes even such small organizations had moments when their allegiance or enmity could tip the scales of an uneasy balance of power. Suk Sark was only one of the "powers" who, for one reason or another, made Korwar their residence, apart from their official headquarters.

"You have a family in the Dipple?" Kyger's abrupt question broke Troy's line of thought.

"No, Merchant."

"Would you take contract, for a limit of time?"

"With you, Merchant?"

"With me. Zul will be of little use for a while. I will need an extra pair of hands in his place. Who knows?" Kyger glanced at him and then away. "It may lead to something better, Dippleman."

"I will take contract, Merchant." Troy schooled his voice, hoping his elation was not too apparent. Somehow he did not wish this spacer-turned-merchant to know just how much that offer meant to him.

They lifted from the square of the crash and took the straightest line to the court at the rear of the shop. Troy was told to load the two crates on a runner and put them in the storeroom. Kyger himself remained by the curtained cage once he had returned the accommodation flitter on auto-control to the rental station. So far he made no move to open the cage, and Troy's desire to see what was inside grew.

"Shall I take this also, Merchant?" Troy asked as he returned and brought the runner to a halt beside the cage.

Kyger turned on him once more the searching stare with which he had measured him at their first meeting that morning. Then the shop owner pulled at some hidden fastening. The padded curtains fell away and Troy looked into a very well-appointed traveling box. The flooring, sides, and roof were padded with plasta-foam, a precaution against the pressure of ship acceleration, and there were two inset feeding and watering niches. But the occupants were close to the mesh front, sitting on their haunches, their front paws placed neatly together, the tips of their tails folded over those paws.

One was black, a black so deep as to have, in the sunlight, a bluish tinge—or perhaps that was a reflection from its companion's coat, for the second and slightly smaller animal *was* blue—or parts of its close, thick fur coat held that shade, muting into a gray that was very dark on head, legs, and tail. And the four eyes of the pair, regarding both men impartially, were as vividly blue-green as aquamarines.

"Terran," Kyger announced with a note of pride plain in his voice. "Terran cats!"

Three

Troy studied the animals. Although those blue eyes regarded him squarely, there was no other contact. Yet he was sure it had not been only his imagination that had stirred him earlier.

Kyger opened the cage. The black cat arose, arched its satin-smooth back, extended forelegs in a luxurious stretch, and then padded out into the courtyard, its blue companion remaining behind while the black scouted with eyes and nose.

"Sooooo—" Kyger subdued his usual authoritative tone into a coaxing murmur and held out his hand for the black to sniff.

Cats were part of the crew of every spaceship. Troy had seen them about the docks. But centuries of such star voyaging must have radically mutated the strain if these were the parent stock. None of those possessed such sleek length of limb, or the sharply pointed muzzle, large, delicately shaped ears, color and rich beauty of fur. He might have compared his own bony, work-scarred hand to the well-kept fingers of a Korwarian villa dweller.

The black leaped, effortlessly, to the top of the cage, and its smaller mate emerged. From that mouth ringed in dark gray came no soft appeal but a sound closer to the ear-shattering wail that had screeched through the flitter before the crash. Kyger laughed.

"Hungry, eh?" He spoke to one of the yardmen. "Bring me a food packet."

Troy watched the merchant break open the sealed container and shake a portion of its contents into the bowls he had loosed from the interior of the cage. The stuff—tough, dry-looking as it sifted down—turned moist and puffy in the dishes. The cats sniffed and then ate decorously.

They were to be Kyger's own charges, Troy discovered, though the shop had a resident staff—two yardmen to tend the cages in the courtyard and some for interior work. Oddly enough, Troy was set to work inside, perhaps taking over some of Zul's tasks.

His shoulder still ached from the bruising impact of the crash, but he tried to satisfy Kyger as the other guided him around, issuing a stream of orders, which at least were concise and easy to obey.

Of the four cage rooms along the corridor between office and show lounges, the first two were for birds, or flying things that might be roughly classed under that heading. Troy had to snatch observations between filling water containers, spreading out a wealth of seeds, exotic fruits, and even bits of meat and fish. The next two chambers were dissimilar. One was filled with tanks and aquariums holding marine dwellers; Troy merely glanced into that since there was a trained tankman on duty. The other was for small animals.

The cats disappeared into Kyger's own office and Troy did not see them again. Nor, as he worked about the cages in the animal room, did he again experience that odd, somewhat disturbing sense of invisible contact. All the creatures were friendly enough, many of them clamoring for his attention, reaching out to him with paws, calling in a whole range of sounds. He was amused, intrigued, attracted—but this was not the same.

He ate his noon rations in the courtyard, apart from Kyger's other employees. C.L. men and subcitizens were never too friendly. And in the midafternoon he witnessed the departure of the Terran cats.

A service robot carried the traveling cage and a food crate at the head of the small procession. Then came a jeweled vision of the hired-companion class, for she swung several small bags on their cords. Next, trailed diffidently by Kyger—if that ex-spacer could ever act a merchant's deference—was a second woman, her features hard to distinguish under the modish painted design of glitter stars on cheek and forehead, the now ultrafashionable "modesty veil" enwrapping mouth, chin, and the rest of her head. Her long coat and tight undertrousers were smartly severe and as unadorned as her companion's were ornately embellished.

As she spoke, her voice held the irremediable lisp of the Lydian-born. And it was plain she was delighted with her new pets. Troy ducked into the door of the fish room to let them pass.

He did not understand why he felt that strange prick of irritation. The Gentle Fem San duk Var was almost the wealthiest consort on Korwar, and the cats had been specially ordered to satisfy her whim. Why did he resent their going? Why? He had had his own piece of luck out of this transaction—the chance that Kyger might keep him on the staff, at least until Zul returned.

Kyger, having seen the party off, called Troy to his office. The com plate on the wall was already activated,

31

and on it was the palm-sized length of white Troy had hardly dared to hope he would ever see.

"Contract"—Kyger was clearly in a hurry to have this done—"to hold a seven-day term. No off-world clause. Suit you, Horan?"

Troy nodded. Even a seven-day contract was to be cherished. He asked only one question. "Renewal for kind?"

"Renewal for kind," the other agreed without hesitation, and Troy's confidence soared. He crossed the small room, set his right hand flat against that glowing plate. "Troy Horan, Norden, class two, accepts contract for seven days, not off-world, from Kyger's," he recited, allowing his hand to remain tight against the heated panel for a full moment before he gave way to Kyger.

The other's hand, wider, the fingers thicker and blunter at the tips, smacked against the white oblong in turn.

"Kossi Kyger, registered merchant, accepts contract for seven days from Troy Horan, laborer. Record it so."

The metallic voice of the recorder chattered back at them. "It is so sealed and noted."

Kyger returned to his eazi-rest. "Shop uniform in the storehouse. Any reason for you to go back to the Dipple tonight?"

Troy paused to shake his head. His few possessions of any value had been thumb-locked into a Dipple safe pocket that morning. And the lock would hold against any touch but his own for ten days. He could pick up the contents of that very small locker any time. Was it imagination again, or did Kyger seem to be relieved?

"Zul furnished night watch inside here. One man

inside, a yardman out, a patroller on alarm call. Some of the stock are delicate. You'll make two rounds—"

He was interrupted by the showroom gong and pulled himself to his feet. "Change and get to work," he ordered as he left the office.

Troy sealed the fore seam of the shop coveralls and strapped on again his rider's belt. The Kyger livery was of the same dark blue that Kyger affected in his own garments, and it did not include the reptileskin boots Zul had worn—nor was there any knife for the belt. He had risen one short step above the Dipple, but that was all.

Shopping hours ran on into the late evening, and twice Troy was summoned to the display rooms to carry in some animate treasure for inspection. He had just returned a squirming cub, listed as an animal but with fluffy feathers instead of fur and six legs waving wildly in the air, a big-eared head digging chin point into Troy's shoulder as it looked with avid interest at the world, to a cage, where three more of its kind immediately fell upon it in mock attack, when Kyger came to the door.

"That closes us for tonight. Guard quarters are next to the storeroom. I'm aloft—over there." He jerked a thumb at the back wall of the courtyard and the line of windows looking out from a second level. "Here—" His hand cupped over a knob of brilliant scarlet just inside the door and now glowing in the subdued light of the cage room. "Need help, hit one of these. There's one in each room. You'll make rounds at three, again at six. Meanwhile"—below the knob was a lever he pushed up—"you'll be able to hear them through the com if there's any disturbance. The yard cages are not your concern."

"Yes, Merchant," Troy assented.

Kyger went on down the corridor, stopping to thumb-seal the door of his office—almost ostentatiously, as if he wanted his most recent employee to witness that act.

Then, without any good night, he was gone. Troy felt the nudge of responsibility. He stepped inside each bird room. The light was dimmed; many of the inhabitants were now asleep. In every room the lever was up, the com safely on. Then he went to the padded wall shelf in the cubby off the storeroom, still a little too excited to sleep.

Within a matter of three days the pattern of Kyger's had become a routine into which Troy fitted easily. He had been successful in caring for a delicate and rare fussel hawk, which Kyger himself had been unable to handle, and had begun to hope that perhaps his week's contract might indeed be renewed. He also discovered that Kyger's not only sold—but bought.

There was a second entrance to the shop through the courtyard, an inconspicuous covered way through which men, mostly wearing spacer uniform, found their way, with either carrying cages or other wild-life containers. All of these, he had his orders, were to be shown directly to Kyger's private office. And should the merchant be busied with customers, a certain signal of gong notes was to be sounded.

At the conclusion of one of these visits Troy, or a yardman, would be summoned to take away a purchase. But the majority of these were sheltered in the yard, not among the rarities of the inner shop. And it appeared to Troy that the number of such sellers did not match the number of visitors—as if some of those

34

unobtrusive men might have visited the ex-spacer for another reason. But that too might have an easy explanation; shipmates from old runs could well drop in while in port. Or there might be still a third reason—one that fitted the attack made upon Zul himself with the interest Varms had shown.

Tikil was a luxury port. And the luxuries were not always within the bands of legal imports. Troy could name four forbidden drugs, a banned liquor, and several other items that would never arrive openly on the planet but would promise high returns for the men or man reckless enough to run them through port scanners. If Kyger had activities outside the port laws, however, that was none of his cage cleaner's concern.

On the fourth afternoon after he had taken contract, Troy was called to the showrooms. Two customers were present, and Kyger's attention had been claimed by the one who, with her party, was in the outer lounge. He waved Horan to the man waiting.

"Show this Gentle Homo the box of tri-dees from Hathor. Yes. Gentle Fem"—the merchant turned back to the glittering party he was serving—"there are many other Terran beasts which one might consider, fully equal in beauty and intelligence to cats. Let me show you—"

When Troy would have led the way to the next lounge, the man he was to assist stopped him with a shake of the head. It appeared that he also wanted to see the wonder Kyger was about to reveal.

The merchant pressed a button. A small viewing screen moved outward from the wall at a comfortable eye level for the woman in the foreseat of the party. She was older than Var's consort, and far more elaborately dressed, affecting the semitransparent robes of Cynus, though they were not in the least flattering to her emaciated figure. Her voice was a shrill caw, but as Troy caught sight of her sharp-featured profile, he knew her for the Grand Leader One from Sidona. That was a matriarchate in name only now, a cluster of three small planets about a dying sun. But it still occupied a strategic point on an important star lane, and what power the Grand Leader Ones might have lost in battle they still possessed in alliances.

"This, Gentle Fem"—Kyger clicked thumb and finger together and was answered by the instant appearance on the screen of a tri-dee—"is a fox. I have already a pair in transit so I can promise an early delivery."

"So?" The Grand Leader One leaned forward a little, the corners of her pinched mouth drawing down to deepen lines from a beak nose. "And how many credits will the coming of such take from my purse, Merchant?"

Kyger named a sum that five days earlier would have made Troy incredulous. Now he merely wondered how long the bargaining would continue.

"A fox, now," the man standing beside him said very softly, his observation hardly above a whisper, as if he were thinking aloud.

The animal in the tri-dee was clearly depicted life-size, the usual procedure for smaller beasts. It had a thick coat of orange-red, black legs and feet, a white tip on its brush of tail. The head was almost triangular with sharp-pointed ears and muzzle, and greenish eyes slanted in that alert and mischievous mask. It was larger than the cats, but its expression of sly intelligence was most marked.

But something in the way his own waiting customer

had said "fox" suggested to Troy that the other was not unacquainted with the Terran exotic. However, he did not linger now but stepped into the second lounge, and Horan had to accompany him.

"I understand you have a fussel hawk."

"That is so, Gentle Homo."

"Have you flown it yet?"

"No, Gentle Homo. The ship passage left it fretful— we have allowed it cage rest."

Those strangely golden eyes flickered to Troy's middle and the wide belt there.

"You are of Norden?"

"I was born there," Troy replied shortly.

"Then you have perhaps already hunted with a fussel."

Troy's lips twitched. "I have seen such hunting. But Norden is many years behind me, Gentle Homo. There was a war." He kept his tone respectful; in fact, he was a little surprised. The stranger had no signs, such as Kyger carried, of being an ex-spacer. Yet not one Korwarian in ten thousand would have recognized Troy's belt, or would have known that the riders of the Norden-that-was had hunted with fussel hawks in the mountain valleys. He studied the other covertly as he made ready the viewing screen.

They were nearly the same height, but the Korwarian was perhaps ten planet years older. He did not have the look of a villa aristocrat, not even of one who played hard and kept his body in top condition. Since he wore no official uniform, he was not a member of any of the three services. Yet plainly he was a man who knew action and the outdoors. His skin must be as fair as Troy's under the even tan of much exposure.

In a concession to fashion he had a braided topknot of hair, banded with two golden hold rings, and that hair was a dull red-gold, not far removed in shade from the metal. His loose tunic and kilt were of a creamy-brown nubb-metalla in which a small golden spark flashed here and there as he moved. There were yellow gems in the hilt of his belt knife and ringing his wrist bracelets, so that the whole effect was that of a golden man, yet did not in any way suggest a villa fop.

"I have not seen you here before. Where is Zul?" There was no arrogance in the question. The stranger asked as if he had a real interest in who might serve him.

"He was injured—there was a flitter smash," Troy replied somewhat evasively, and then added with the strict truth, "I am C.L., on a fill-time contract."

"From the Dipple?" The other gave the name none of the accent that had made that place of abode a fighting word in Tikil. "Well, and what has Kyger got to offer in his Hathor tri-dees?"

He seated himself at last, waving aside the selection of smoke sticks and drinks Troy offered. Horan snapped the button and the first of the views flashed on the screen. It was apparent from the series that this would-be customer was interested only in birds of prey that could be trained for the hunt. But when Troy had run through the entire Hathor collection, the man shook his head.

"When one knows there is a fine weapon within reach, one does not pick up the second best. If Kyger has a fussel worth training, I shall not order from these." Now he did pick a smoke stick, struck it against his fingernail to set it burning with its herb-scented smoke. "Ah, Kyger!" He looked up as the merchant entered. "And did you make that stellar sale? How long will the august mother of three worlds have to wait for her new toy?"

There was something in the lounge, as invisible as the touch from the cats' cage. This was a tenseness, the faintest possible suggestion of strain. Yet both men were outwardly at ease. Kyger seated himself in another chair as if there were no barriers of rank between them.

"Not too long. I have a pair arriving on the Shammor."

"So? Gambling in Terran imports now, Kyger?"

The ex-spacer shrugged. "They want to build up their export trade—and they are willing to pare prices to open a new market. My friends on the ships pass the word—"

His customer nodded. "Yes. Well, trade makes ties to defeat war. And if you can get the Terrans well tied up, you'll have the smiles of the Council, Kyger."

Again that flash of feeling. Troy could not be sure which man was involved. The golden man stubbed out his smoke stick.

"You have a fussel—"

Kyger picked up a refreshment bulb, squeezed its contents into his mouth. "I have. It'll have to prove itself in flight, though, before I market it."

"Just so. I am due to make an inspection trip through the Wild. Trust me with that testing—send along your man here."

Kyger glanced at Horan. "All right. He knows how to handle the bird, uncrated it when the rest of us couldn't get near. Very well, Hunter. When do you wish to leave, and for how long?"

"Three days to be gone. I must swing up as far as the Marches. As to when—well, shall we say in two days? That will give your bird that much longer to rest before we take him out."

Kyger crushed the beverage bulb in one hand. "Agreed. You," he said to Troy, "will hold yourself ready for the Hunter Rerne's orders."

The golden man left, walking with an almost soundless tread that Troy did not now find surprising. Kyger continued to sit for a long moment, his eyes still on the door through which the other had gone.

"Rerne." He repeated that name very softly. If there was any expression in his tone, Troy failed to read it.

The Hunters, the rangers of the Wild, were conservation experts. Guardians of the vast sections of carefully preserved forest and unsettled lands, into which parties of visitors or the villa dwellers of Korwar might be guided to enjoy the thrills of primitive living while still in flyer touch with the safety and luxury of civilization, they were almost legendary in Tikil. And the office had become, through two centuries, hereditary, going to the members of some ten or twelve families, all of them First-Ship pioneers on Korwar.

Rerne's Clan lived to the north. And this man, because of his youth, must be one of the two brothers whose discovery of the ill-fated Fauklow expedition was still something of a saga in the port city. Troy fingered the belt from which no knife hung. Even a subcitizen could seldom hope for a chance to penetrate the Wild. The trackers, foresters, woodsmen themselves all came of lesser families allied by old ties to the Clans. Yet he was going with Rerne in two days' time!

Four

The news flash came during the slack time at the shop. Those visitors who favored the afternoon had gone, and the evening strollers were not yet abroad. Kyger had retreated to his office; his employees gathered for their evening meal. Troy balanced a plate on his knee in the courtyard. Through the window vent over his head he could hear the mechanical recitation of the day's events over Kyger's com.

"—the so-far unexplainable and sudden death of Sattor Commander Varan Di."

Troy stopped chewing. Two feet away stood the flitter, and right now there was a box resting in it intended for the hillside villa of Sattor Commander Varan Di, a special shipment of food for the Commander's pet.

"—resigned from the overlordship of the Council during the previous year," continued the drone from within. "But his years of experience led him to agree to continue as consultant on special problems. It is rumored that he was acting at present as adviser on the terms of the Treaty of Panarc Five. This has been neither confirmed nor denied by government spokesmen. Statement issued by the Council: 'It is with deep regret—' "

The monotone of the com snapped into a silence, the more noticeable because of that sudden break. Troy went on eating. The death, "unexplainable and sudden" as the com had it, of a retired military leader and former Council lord now had very little to do with Troy Horan. Ten years ago—again Troy's hand paused on its way to his mouth—ten years ago matters might have been different. It had been Varan Di who had arbitrarily decided to make a military depot for Sattor-class ships out of Norden. Not that that made any difference now.

"Horan!" Kyger came to the courtyard entrance. Troy put down his plate, noting small signs of irritation in his employer. "Take the flitter up to the Di villa and deliver that package."

Well, Troy supposed, eating, even for a pet, went on when the master was dead. But why the rush to send him now—and why him at all? The yardman usually took the flitter out on such errands. But this was no time to ask questions. He folded his long legs into the driver's seat, made a creditable lift from the courtyard.

The journey tape had already been set for the trip; he had nothing to do but take off and land, and be ready to assume manual control if any remote emergency arose. In the meantime he settled back in the cramped seat to enjoy this small time of privacy and ease.

The golden haze, which was Korwar's fair-weather sky, somehow reminded him of Rerne and the promised trip into the Wild. Troy had taken time twice that afternoon, after the Hunter had left, to visit the fussel. And on the second inspection the big bird had stirred on his perch and stretched his wings, which was a very encouraging sign. The fussel was male, perhaps two years old, so just entering the best training age.

42

Wild as he had been when loosed from the traveling cage, he had not struck at Troy, as he had attempted to do at both Kyger and the assisting yardman, which could—or might—mean that the bird would be willing to ride with Horan.

"Lane warning—lane warning!" The words spat from the mike on the control board, a light flashing in additional emphasis.

Troy looked up. A patroller hung poised, as the fussel might poise, over the flitter, ready to swoop for the kill.

"Identify yourself!" came the order Troy expected.

He pushed the button that would report to the law the destination and reason for the errand as it appeared on his journey tape, expecting instructions to take manuals and sheer off. If the patrollers were investigating a suspicious death, they would not allow him to set down at the Di villa.

But surprisingly enough he was told to proceed. Nor was he challenged again as the flitter settled before the service quarters of the late Sattor Commander's mountainside retreat.

Like all Korwar aristocrats, Varan Di had constructed a dwelling on a plan native to another world, choosing for a model the stark simplicity of the Pa-ta-du of the sea mountains of Qwan. Even a growth of pink-gray lace bushes could not disguise the rugged wall posts, though their softening color was reflected by the sheets of barmush shell that formed the wall surfaces between those posts. Troy tried to estimate the number of credits that must have been spent to import posts, shell sheets, and doubtless all the rest from across stellar space. And he doubted if it all

43

could have been done on the legal pay of either a sattor commander or a Council lord's post.

He pulled the case of food out of the flitter, shouldered it, and turned toward the delivery port of the villa. Men were moving in the garden, patrollers' uniforms very much in evidence. Their attention appeared to be centered on a small structure half hidden by an artificial grouping of plume trees, a structure as architecturally different from the villa it accompanied as the fussel was from a bob-chit. In place of shell-post walls, translucent, this was a solid block of stone, cut and set with precision, but also giving the impression of a primitive erection from some prespace-flight civilization thousands of years removed in time from the larger house.

A man came out of its doorway, and Troy stopped short. Just as the invisible touch of exploration had alerted him in the warehouse, so now did a feeling within him answer a new, voiceless cry for help. The sensation of terror and, beyond that terror, the breathless need to convey some vital information struck into his mind almost as a physical blow. And without conscious thinking he answered that plea with an unvoiced query in return: "What—where—how—?"

The man who had come from the stone-walled garden house twisted and made a grab into the air as something wriggled from his clutch and sprang into the nearest plume tree. Only an agitation of foliage marked its path from there to the villa—or was it toward Troy? A tree branch bobbed and from it a small body flung itself in a crazy leap through the air.

Troy put down the box just in time to take the shock of that weight landing on his shoulder. A prehensile
44

tail curled about his neck, small legs clutched him frenziedly, and he put up an arm to enfold a small, trembling, softly furred animal. A round, broad head butted against him, as if the creature were trying to ball into a refuge. Troy stroked the thick yellow-brown fur soothingly.

"Kill—" No one had spoken that word aloud; it flashed into his mind, and with it a wavering, oddly shaped picture of a man crumpled in a chair. Troy shook his head and the picture was gone. But the fear in the animal in his arms remained alive and strong.

"Danger—" Yes, that got across. Danger not only for the creature he held, but for others—men—

The man who had lost this animal was hurrying forward, and two of the patrollers also made their way purposefully toward Troy. In that same moment he knew that he intended to protect the thing he held, even against the weight of Korwar's law.

"Sooooo—" He made the same soothing sound Kyger had used with the cats, stroking the furred back gently. The butting of the head against his chest was now not so violent. And Troy tried to establish a contact promising protection and aid. What he was doing, or why and how he could do it, did not matter now—that he was able to establish the contact did.

"Who are you?"

Troy settled the still-shivering animal more firmly into the hollow between shoulder and arm and looked with very little favor at his questioner. "Horan." He pointed with his chin at the flitter, with the shop name clearly lettered on its body. "From Kyger's."

One of the patrollers cleared his throat and then spoke with a deferential note that suggested the importance of the civilian interrogating Troy. "That's the animal and bird importer, Gentle Homo. I believe that the Sattor Commander purchased this thing there—"

The man he addressed was harsh-faced, flat-eyed. He stared at Troy as if he presented some very elemental problem that could be speedily solved—not particularly to the problem's advantage.

"What are you doing here?"

Troy touched with the toe of his boot the box he had just set down. "Delivery, Gentle Homo. Special food for the Commander's pet."

The flat-eyed man looked to the second patroller and that individual nodded. "It was referenced for today, Gentle Homo. Special imported food for the—the—" He hesitated over the unfamiliar name before he offered it. "The kinkajou."

"The what?" his superior demanded. "What kind of an outlandish, other-sun thing—?"

"It is Terran, Gentle Homo," his second underling answered with a small flash of importance. "Very rare. The Sattor Commander was quite excited about it."

"Kinkajou—Terran—" The officer advanced a step or two as he tried to see more of the animal clinging to Troy. "But what was it doing rummaging through the Sattor Commander's desk if it is just an animal? Do you have an answer for that?"

"Danger!" Troy did not need that flash of warning from the creature in his arms. It was plain to read in the whole stance of the man before him.

"Many animals are very curious, Gentle Homo." Troy sought to divert the officer. "Do not Korwarian kattans open any package they can lay claws upon?"
46

The voluble patroller was nodding assent to that. And Troy pushed a little further. "Animals also imitate the actions of men with whom they are closely associated, Gentle Homo. The kinkajou may have been following the routine of the Sattor Commander. What else could it be? Surely it would not be doing so for a purpose—" But, Troy guessed now, that must have been what the creature was doing when caught. Did this officer have more exact knowledge of that fact?

"Possible," the other conceded. "Just to make sure that there shall be no more such mischief, you will take this kinkajou with you and return it to Kyger. He shall be responsible for it until the investigation into the Sattor Commander's death is completed. Tell him the Commandant of the West Sector orders it."

"It is done, Gentle Homo."

Troy tried to put the kinkajou into the flitter first, before he replaced the box. But the animal refused to loose its hold upon him. In addition, rising above the fear it conveyed to him, there was again that urgency, an urgency that was clearly connected with the stone house in the garden. The kinkajou wanted him to return it to that building until it finished some task, protecting it meanwhile from his own kind. But to that he dared not agree. For the first time the animal gave tongue, uttering sharp, chittering cries, as if so it could enforce the volume of their silent communication.

"Get aloft!"

The Commandant had gone back to the garden house, and the patrollers moved in on Troy. He had no wish to have them turn ugly. Somehow he managed to tip the box back into the flitter, the kinkajou protesting the retreat bitterly—though Troy noted it made no attempt to leave him.

Once they were aloft again, the animal quieted down, apparently accepting defeat. Seated in Troy's lap, its tail curled about one of his arms as if for reassurance and support, it surveyed the world of the sky through which they flew with what might have been taken for intelligent interest. But it made no more attempts to reason with him.

When the flitter set down in the court of Kyger's establishment, the kinkajou moved to the cabin door, patted it with front paws, and looked to Troy entreatingly, every line of its rounded body expressing eagerness to be free. He caught at the prehensile tail, having no wish to see the creature escape by one of its spectacular leaps. Leaving the flyer and grasping his indignant captive firmly, Troy went toward his employer's office.

Kyger appeared at the corridor door, and when he saw the squirming animal in Troy's hold, he halted nearly in midstep. Again Troy caught that spark of unease which he had detected in the meeting between the ex-spacer and Rerne.

"What happened?" Kyger's tone was as usual. He stepped back into his office and Troy accepted the tacit invitation to enter. The escape attempts of the kinkajou were at an end again. Once more the animal pushed against Horan's chest as if in mute plea for protection. But the mental contact had utterly ceased.

Swiftly and tersely, as a serviceman giving a report to a superior officer, Troy outlined what had happened at the Di villa. But he made no mention of the odd contact with the Kinajou. He had early learned in the hard school of the Dipple that knowledge could be both a weapon and a defense, and something as nebulous and beyond reason as his odd mental meeting with two different species of Terran life he preferred to keep to himself—at least until he knew Kyger better.

Kyger made no move to separate the clinging animal from Horan but sat down in the eazi-rest. His fingers rubbed up and down the scar seam from his ear.

"That's a valuable specimen," he remarked mildly when Troy had done. "You were right to bring it back here. Curious as a ffolth sand borer. There was no reason for the law to upset it to the point of hysteria! Put it in the empty end cage in the animal room, give it some water and a few quagger nuts, and leave it alone."

Troy followed orders, but once at the cage he had some difficulty in detaching the kinkajou. The animal appeared to accept Horan as a refuge in the midst of a chancy world, and he had to pry paws and tail loose from their hold on him. As he closed the cage door, the captive rolled itself into a tight ball in the corner farthest from the light, presenting only a stubborn hump of furred back to the world.

During the few days he had been at Kyger's, Troy had come to look forward to the early hours of the night when he was left alone in the interior of the main buildings. He made two watch rounds according to his orders. But each night before he napped, he had his own visiting pattern. The fussel hawk, the blue-feathered cubs that always greeted him with reaching paws and joyous squeaks, and several other favorites were then his alone. Tonight he came also to the kinkajou cage. From the appearance of that furred ball still wedged into the corner, the creature had not moved from the position it had assumed when he first put it there.

Deliberately Troy tried mental contact, suggesting friendship, a desire for better understanding. But if the kinkajou received those suggestions, it neither acknowledged nor reacted to them. Disappointed, Troy left the room after setting the com broadcaster.

When he stretched out on his bunk, he tried to fit one event of the day to another. But when he remembered Rerne and the other's request for his services in testing the fussel in the Wild, Troy drifted into a daydream, which, in a very short interval, became a real dream.

Troy rolled over, his shoulder bringing up against the wall with a smart rap, his head turning fretfully. There was a thickness behind his eyes, which was not quite a pressure of pain, only a dull throb. He opened his eyes. The dial of the timekeeper faced him, and the hour marked there was well past the middle of the night—though not quite time for his round. But as long as he was now thoroughly awake, he might as well make it.

He sat up, pulled on his half boots. Then he pressed his fingertips gently to his temples. The dull feeling in his head persisted, and it was not normal. In fact—

Troy's hand flashed to the niche above the head of his bunk, scooping up the weapon that lay waiting there.

Though he had never experienced that particular form of attack before, his wits were now alert enough to supply him with one possible explanation. With the stunner in his hand, he walked as noiselessly as he could to the doorway, peered out into the subdued lighting of the corridor.

To his right was Kyger's office, thumb-sealed as usual. And there had been no betraying sound from the com. No betraying *sound!* But a lack of normal sounds can be as enlightening. Troy had become accustomed to the small twitters, clicks, chattering subcomplaints of the night hours—a myriad of sounds, that issued normally from the cage rooms.

The dull pressure in his own head, together with the absence of those same twitters, clicks, chatters, spelled only one thing. There was a "sleeper" in operation somewhere on the premises—the illegal gadget that could lull into unconsciousness living things not shielded from its effect on the middle ear. And a sleeper was not the tool of a man who had any legitimate business here. It must be turned low enough to handle the animals but not to stun Horan himself into unconsciousness—why?

Troy tested Kyger's sealed office doorway with one hand, the stunner ready in the other. The panel refused to move, so at least that lock had not been forced. He slipped along the wall, paused by the tank room. The gurgle of flowing water, the plop of an aquarium inhabitant—nothing else. The marine things appeared not to have succumbed to the sleeper either.

Horan crossed to the animal room. Again no sound at all—which was doubly suspicious. Inside that door was the alert signal, which would arouse the yardmen and ring straight through to Kyger's quarters. Troy edged about the mesh door, his back against the wall, his free hand going to that knob, ready to push it flat.

"Danger!"

Again that word burst in his brain with the force of a full-lunged scream in his ear. He half turned, and a blast of pure, flaming energy cut so close that he cried out involuntarily at the searing bite of its edge against the line of his chin. Half blinded by the recent glare, Troy snapped the stunner beam at the dark shape arising from the floor and threw himself in a roll halfway across the room.

Troy shot another beam at a black blot in the doorway. But the paralyzing ray seemed to have no effect in even slowing up his attacker. Before Troy could find his feet, the other had made the corridor, and Troy heard the metallic clang of the outer door. Horan stumbled across the room, slammed his hand upon the alarm signal, heard the clamor tear the unnatural silence of the cage room to shreds. Perhaps the aroused yard guard would be able to catch the fugitive now in the open.

Five

The fact that there was no corresponding uproar from the cage rooms confirmed Troy's belief that a sleeper had been set within the shop walls. He turned up the light power to full strength and began a careful search of the room. This was where the intruder had been occupied; what he had sought must lie here.

In the cages the occupants were balled, or sprawled,

in deep, beam-induced slumber, save for that corner cage where the kinkajou had been put. Bright beads of eyes peered out at Troy, small paws rested against the netting. Troy gained an impression of excitement rather than fear. The signal of danger had been meant as a warning to him, not a cry for assistance such as the animal had made in the villa garden.

Troy ran his finger down the netting, looked into those round eyes. "If you could just tell me what is behind all this," he half whispered.

"Someone comes—"

The kinkajou retreated. Before Troy's eyes it rolled quickly into its chosen ball-in-the-corner position once again. Troy's boot struck against some object on the floor, sent it to rebound from the wall with a metallic "ping." He wriggled halfway under the rack of cages and picked up a dull-green cube—the sleeper.

He glanced once more at the kinkajou. To all appearances that animal was now as deeply under the influence of the gadget he held as all the other beasts in the room.

But if the stock of Kyger's establishment had been so subdued, the human inhabitants of the building were not. Two yardmen, stunners in fist, came through into the corridor. And Kyger ran in their wake, his chosen weapon a far more deadly hand blaster, which must be a relic of his service days.

Troy held out the sleeper cube, told his story of the assailant who had appeared so totally immune to the direct fire of a stunner.

"Wearing a person-protect, probably," Kyger snapped impatiently. "Anything gone here—or disturbed—?"

He passed down the line of cages, but as he reached

53

the end one, he paused and gave a searching glance at the ball of sleeping kinkajou. Troy made no mention of the fact that the animal had been able to defy the wave of the sleeper, had saved his own life by its warning. In spite of Kyger's treatment of him, some deep-buried and undefinable emotion kept him from warming to the merchant as he had to Rerne. He had no idea what could lie behind the invasion of the shop, but he wanted to know more of what was going on here.

"I could not see anything wrong," he reported.

Kyger had turned, was walking back along the cages, and his fingers rasped across the netting of the one that held the kinkajou. The ball of fur remained unstirring. As the merchant joined Troy once more, he caught the younger man's chin, turning his head directly to the light.

"You have a flash burn there." His tone was almost accusing.

"He was armed with a blaster," Troy explained.

"What is going on here?"

The yardmen in the doorway were elbowed aside; a patroller came in, blaster ready. Kyger answered with a bite in his voice.

"We had a visitor, who brought this—" He nodded to the sleeper cube on the top of a cage. The patroller scooped it up, his eyes cold.

"What is the damage?"

Kyger's hand fell from Troy's chin to his shoulder. He held that grip, propelling the younger man before him down the corridor.

"So far none, except a flash burn—too close for comfort. Mangy! Tansvel!" The yardmen snapped to
54

attention. "Check out the rest of the rooms; report to me in the office. This officer"—Kyger nodded to the patroller—"will help you."

Troy stood quietly as his employer patted cov-aid dressing along the line of the burn. "Just grazed you." Kyger retopped the container. "You were lucky."

"It was dark and he was off orbit."

But Kyger was watching him with an intent stare as if he could see straight into Troy's memory and pick out the events as they had really happened—the incredible fact that a warning had struck from an animal's mind to his.

"He must have been badly jigged," Kyger commented. "So much so that I wonder. A sleeper makes this a Guild job—and I have one or two unfriends around here who might just employ such means to make trouble for me." He was frowning a little. "Only Guild men do not get jigged—"

"A novice might."

Kyger spread both hands on the top of his desk. "A novice? What do *you* know about this, Horan?"

"I noticed a new buy-in man at the warehouse before they tried to lift us on the street." Troy trusted now to Kyger's own background. To a merchant-born he would not have made such an admission, unless the matter had proved far more serious than it was. But to a spacer who had himself lived by a more flexible code of ethics—or rather, a different code of ethics—he could confess that much.

"A proving job for a novice." Kyger considered that. "Might fit this flight pattern, at that. This buy-in man knows you?"

"He saw me at the warehouse—just as I saw him."

55

"Any challenge between you two?"

"If you mean was this personal—no. He was Dipple and I knew him by name, but we never messed together."

"Silly jig, hitting here. Unless it was just for nuisance value. There is nothing he could pick up to trot to the pass-boys."

Troy wondered about that himself. Portable property was to be had for the ingenious lifts of the Guild anywhere in Tikil, where theft had become both a business and a fine art. Why would anyone try to lift living creatures, most of which required special food and attention? There was only one possibility.

"Some one-of-a-kind already promised?" he hazarded, knowing Kyger's promises to his elite customers. A unique pet, certified to the the only one of its kind on Korwar, might be an inducement.

"No profit in that. It would have to be kept under cover." Kyger put his finger on the weakness in that. Yes, the value of such a pet to the vain owner would be largely in its display before the envious.

"To keep someone else from having it?"

Again that disconcerting stare from Kyger. Troy thought he had found another small piece in this match puzzle. That had hit, if not straight to the heart of the target, reasonably near.

"Might be. That makes a spot more sense. You can bunk in. I might cover the rest of the night watch."

That was straight dismissal. Troy went back to his bunk, this time easing out of his clothes. The dressing had taken most of the smart out of his burn. But his mind was active and he did not feel in the least inclined to sleep. He closed his eyes, trying to will relaxation.

Instead, as if some tenuous circle of thought had coiled out into the air—as Lang Horan's rupan rope had done so accurately years before to catch and hold a twisting, bucking quarry—Troy's heightened sensitivity touched and held something never intended to join more than one pair of minds under that roof this night.

"He died quick. No time to see the report before put away—"

"Must return!" That was an order, final and harsh.

"Not so. No good. Man saw Shang look for report. Was suspicious!"

"There must be no suspicion!" Again the harshness.

And now there was no more protest in words, rather a thread of fear, a thread that grew into a choking rope. Troy's eyes opened. He sat up on the bunk, alive and vibrating to that fear as if its force raged in him also.

But if there was fear in that band of communication, there was also something else he recognized—a determination to fight. And to that his sympathy responded.

"If there is suspicion, there will be questions."

Silence from the harsh one. Was that marking thoughtful consideration of the argument? Or rejection of its validity? Troy's hands were sweat-wet and now his fingers clenched into fists. If what he suspected was true— The kinkajou and Kyger? But why? How? Terran animals able to communicate being used for a set purpose? Yet Kyger was no Terran—or was he? Troy himself was too ignorant of other worlds, except for the people of the Dipple, to make a positive identification. He remembered Kyger's own questions about his past on the day he had been hired.

Terra was the center of the Confederation—or had been before the war. But she had not come out well at the end of that conflict; too many of her allies had gone down to defeat. From the dominant voice she had sunk to a second-rate, even third-rate, power at the conference tables. The Council and the Octed of the Rim maneuvered for first power, while the old Confederation had fractured into at least three collections of smaller rulerships. His thoughts were broken once more by that unidentifiable thought stream—again the master voice: "Who came tonight?"

"One who knew nothing. He was an enemy outside the scheme. There was no touch."

"Yet he could have been hired by another. Traps need bait."

Troy read the thought behind that last. So—if he were right and it was the kinkajou and Kyger who were talking so—then such an animal might well be stolen to serve as bait for its master.

But why had not the animal reported Troy's ability to receive the mind touch, if not with the ease and clarity of this exchange, then after a fashion? Or did the kinkajou, fearing its master, hold Troy in reserve as a possible escape, as he had been for it at the Di villa?

"An enemy outside the scheme!" The master voice picked that up now. "Against me?"

"Against you," the kinkajou (if it was that) agreed. "He was paid to cause trouble, bring you into the shop that he might kill—"

"Kill." That word throbbed in Troy's head. He strained to catch an answer. But there was no more that night. At last he slept fitfully, awaking now and then to lie silent, listening not only with his ears but with the portion of his brain that had tapped the exchange. But save for the sound of the birds and animals coming out of the daze of the sleeper to their normal nocturnal restlessness, he heard nothing on either plane of the senses.

In the morning, after the general round of cage tending and feeding was over, Kyger summoned Troy to the fussel hawk. The big bird was definitely emerging from its sullenness of the landing. It held its crested head high, turned it alertly from side to side. Still young enough to have some of its adolescent tail plumage, it was yet a strikingly beautiful bird with its brilliant, iridescent-black rakish crest above its bright golden head, back-patched by warrior scarlet. The golden glow of breast and the scarlet of back were blended on the strongly pinioned wings to a warm orange beneath which the darker tail and black legs again made contrast. But it was not for beauty alone that the fussel was esteemed.

On countless worlds—human, humanoid, and even nonhuman—intelligences had trained birds of falcon and hawklike strains to be hunter-companions. And now when the highly civilized were returning to more primitive skills and amusements for pleasure, hunting —not with high-power kill weapons, but with hawk or other trained birds and animals—was well established. The fussel—with its intelligence, its ability to be easily trained through the right handling, and its power to capture rather than kill a quarry upon demand—was a highly valued item of sale for any trainer.

Now, seeing the stance of the bird, Troy drew his fingers slowly, enticingly, across the front of the cage.

Unlike its attitude of only two days earlier, it made no lighning stab to punish such impudence. Instead, deep in its throat, the bird gave a sound of interested inquiry and moved along the perch toward the door opening of the cage as if awaiting release.

"Shall I man him?" Troy asked.

Kyger snapped his fingers at the opposite side of the cage. That act, which had brought the fussel into raging battle before, now only led it to turn its head. Then it looked back again expectantly at the cage door.

"Here." Kyger tossed the hawker's glove to Troy. As the latter drew it on, the fussel uttered its soft cry, this time with a half-coaxing note.

Horan loosened the door, extended protected hand and wrist into the cage. The fussel ducked its head, not to stab, but to draw its curved beak along the tough fabric of the glove. Then sedately it moved from perch to wrist, and Troy carefully lifted the bird out into the open of the corridor into which they had moved the cage for this experiment.

"Olllahuuu!"

Both men turned quickly at the Hunter's call of appreciation. Rerne stood there, smiling a little.

"Your friend here looks eager for a casting," he remarked.

The fussel mantled, raising wings wide in display, shaking them a little as if glad to be free of the cage. The clawhold on Troy's wrist was firm, and the bird gave no sign of wanting to quit that post.

"Truly a beauty," Rerne complimented Kyger. "If he performs as well as he looks, you have already made a sale, Merchant."

"He is yours to try, Gentle Homo."

"When better than now? It seems that there is an earlier demand for my services in the Wild than I had thought. I am come one day ahead of time to claim this man of yours and the bird."

Kyger made no protest. In fact the speed with which he equipped Troy with the loan of a camp kit and the affability with which he saw them both away from the shop made Horan uneasy. He had had no chance to visit the kinkajou alone. And when he had been engaged in cage cleaning earlier that day, Kyger or one of the yardmen had been in and out of the room and the animal had remained in its tight ball. He wished that he could have taken it with him, but there was no possible way of explaining such a request. And he had to leave with a small doubt—of what he could not honestly have said—still worrying him.

Rerne's flitter was strictly utilitarian, though with compact storage space and the built-in necessities for a flyer that might also provide a temporary camp shelter in the wilderness. Oddly enough he had no pilot, and when Troy, with the fussel again in the transport cage, climbed into the passenger compartment, he found no other but the Hunter awaiting him there. Nor did Rerne prove talkative. His city finery was gone with his city manners. Now he wore soft hide breeches, made of some dappled skin, pale fawn and white, and tanned to suppleness of fabric. His jerkin was of the same, sleeveless and cut low on the chest so his own golden-tanned skin showed in a wide V close to the same shade as the garment. The rings of precious metal that had held his hair had been traded for thongs confining the locks as tightly but far

61

more inconspicuously. And about his waist was a belt, plain of any jeweled ornament, but supporting stunner, bush knife, and an array of small tools and gadgets, each in its own loop.

Under his expert control the flitter spiraled well up above the conventional traffic lanes between villas and city and headed northeast. Beneath them carefully tended gardens or as carefully nurtured "wild" gardens grew farther and farther apart. And as they topped a mountain range, they put behind them all the year-around residences of Tikil. There was a scattering of holiday houses and hunting lodges in the stretch before they came to the Mountains of Larsh—and the territory below, as uninhabited as it looked, was still under the dominion of man.

But beyond the Larsh, into the real Wild, then man's hand lay far lighter. The Hunting Clans had deliberately kept it so and profited thereby. Through the years they had made a mystery of the Wild, and now no one ventured without their guidance past the Larsh.

In the cabin of the flitter the quiet was suddenly broken by a call from the fussel—a cry that held a demand. As Troy tried to sooth the captive, Rerne spoke for the first time since they had taken off: "Try him out of the cage."

Troy was doubtful. If the hawk would refuse the wrist, take to wing, or try to, in this confined space, that action would make for trouble. On the other hand, if the bird was to be of any use in the future, it must learn to accept such transportation free of the cage. A fussel caged too much lost spirit. He pulled on his glove, offered his wrist through the half-open door, and felt the firm grip of the talons through the fabric.

Carefully he brought his arm across his knees, the fussel resting quietly, though its crested head turned from side to side as it eyed the cabin and the open skies beyond the bubble of their covering. As it showed no disquiet, Troy relaxed a little, enough to glance himself at that rising wall of saw-toothed peaks which was the Larsh, gnawing at the afternoon sky.

They did not fly directly across that barrier range. Instead Rerne turned more to the north so that they followed along its broken wall. And they had covered at least an hour's flying time on that course before they took a gateway of a pass between two grim peaks and saw before them a hazy murk hiding the other world Tikil knew little about.

Rerne sent the flitter spiraling down, now that they were across the heights. There was a raveling of lesser peaks and foothills, bright-green streaks marking at least two rivers of some size. Troy leaned against the bubble, trying to see more of the spread beneath. There appeared to be a fog rising with the coming of evening, a thick scum of stuff closing between the flitter and the ground.

With a mutter of impatience, the Hunter again altered course northward. And they had not gone very far before a light flashed red on his control board. When they continued on their path without any deviation, those flashes grew closer together so that the light seemed hardly to blink at all.

"Warn off!" The words were clipped, with a patroller's snap—though the law of Tikil did not operate east of the Larsh.

Rerne spoke into his own mike. "Acknowledge warn off. This is Rernes' Donerabon."

"Correct. Warn off withdrawn," replied the com.

Troy longed to ask a question. And then Rerne spoke, not to the mike, but to his seatmate. "To your right—watch now as we make the crossover."

The flitter dipped, sideslipped down a long descent. There were no streamers of mist to hide the ground here. No vegetation either. In curdled expanse of rock and sand was a huddle of structures, unmistakably, even from this distance, not the work of nature.

Troy studied them avidly. "What is that?"

"Ruhkarv—the 'accursed place.'"

Six

They did not pass directly over that outcropping of alien handiwork, older than the first human landing on Korwar, but headed north once more. Troy knew from reports that what he saw now as lumpy protuberances aboveground were only a fraction of the ruins themselves, as they extended in corridors and chambers layers deep and perhaps miles wide under the surface, for Ruhkarv had never been fully explored.

"The treasure—" he murmured.

Beside him Rerne laughed without any touch of humor. "If that exists outside vivid imaginations, it is never going to be found. Not after the end of the Fauklow expedition."

They had already swept past the open land that

held the ruins, were faced again by the wealth of vegetation that ringed the barren waste of Ruhkarv. And Troy was struck by that oddity of the land.

"Why the desert just about the ruins?" he asked, too interested in what he saw to pay the usual deference to the rank of his pilot.

"That is something for which you will find half-a-dozen explanations," Rerne returned, "any one of them logical—and probably wrong. Ruhkarv exists as it always has since the First-Ship exploration party charted it two centuries ago. Why it continues to exist is something Fauklow may have discovered—before he and his men went mad and killed themselves or each other."

"Did their recaller work?"

Rerne answered obliquely. "The tracer of the rescue party registered some form of wave broadcast—well under the surface—when they came in. They blanketed it at once when they saw what had happened to Fauklow and the others they were able to find. All Ruhkarv is off limits now—under a tonal barrier. No flitter can land within two miles of the only known entrance to the underways. We do pick up some empty-headed treasure hunter now and then, prowling about, hunting a way past the barrier. Usually a trip to our headquarters and enforced inspection of the tri-dees we took of Fauklow's end instantly cures his desire to go exploring."

"If the recaller worked—" Troy speculated as to what might have happened down in those hidden passages. Fauklow had been a noted archaeologist with several outstanding successes at re-creating prehuman civilizations via the recaller, a machine still partially in the experimental stage. Planted anywhere within a structure that had once been inhabited by sentient beings, it could produce—under the right conditions—certain shadowy "pictures" of scenes that had once occurred at the site well back in time. While authorities still argued over dating, over the validity of some of the scenes Fauklow had recorded, yet the most skeptical admitted that he had caught something out of the past. And oftentimes those wispy ghosts appearing on his plates or films were the starting point for new and richly rewarding investigation.

The riddle of Ruhkarv had drawn him three years earlier. While men had prowled the upper layers of the underground citadel, they had found nothing except bare corridors and chambers. The Council had willingly granted Fauklow permission to try out the recaller, with prudent contracts and precautions about securing to Korwar the possession of any outstanding finds that might result from the use of his machine. But the real answer had been a bloody massacre, the details of which were never made public. Men who had worked together for years as a well-running team had seemingly, by the evidence, gone stark mad and created a horror.

"If the recaller worked," Rerne answered, "it did so too well. The mop-up crew did not locate it—so the thing must have been planted well down. And no one hunted it there. It was shorted anyway as soon as we guessed what had happened. Ah—there is our beacon."

Through the gathering twilight the quick flash of a ground light shone clearly. Rerne circled, set the flitter down neatly on a pocket of landing field within a fringe of towering tree giants that effectively shut off the paling gold of the sky except just over the heads of the disembarking men. The fussel on Troy's wrist fanned wings and uttered a new cry, not guttural in the throat, but pealing up a range of notes.

Rerne laughed. "To work, eh, feathered brother? Wait until the dawning and we shall give you strong winds to ride. That is a true promise."

Two men stepped from between the trunks of the tree wall. Like Rerne, they were leather-clad, and in addition one had a long hunting bow projecting beyond his shoulder. They glanced briefly at Troy but had more attention for the bird on his wrist.

"From Kyger's." Without other greeting Rerne indicated the fussel. "And this is Troy Horan who has the manning of him."

Again each of the foresters favored him with a raking glance that seemed, in an instant's space, to classify him.

"To the fire, to the fireside, be welcome." The elder of the two gave a strictly impersonal twist to what was evidently a set formula of welcome. Troy was aware that in this world he was an interloper, to be tolerated because of the man who brought him.

And while he had long known and accepted Tikil's evaluation of the Dipple dwellers, yet here this had a power to hurt, perhaps the more so because of the different attitude Rerne had shown. Now the Hunter came to his aid again.

"A rider from Norden," he said quietly with no traceable inflection of rebuke in his voice, "will always be welcome to the fireside of the 'Donerabon.' "

But inside Troy there was still a smart. "Norden's plains have no riders now." He pointed out the truth. "I am a Dippleman, Gentle Homo."

"There are plains in a man's mind," Rerne replied obscurely. "Leave the fussel uncaged if he will ride easy. We shelter in the Five League Post tonight."

There was a trail between the trees ringing in the landing clearing, firm enough to be followed in the half-light. Yet Troy was certain that the three men of the Wild ranger patrol could have found it in the pitch-darkness. It led steadily up slope until outcrops of rock broke through the clumps of brush and the thinning stands of trees, and they came out on a broad ledge hanging above the end of a small lake.

The lodge was not set on that ledge, but in the cliff wall backing it. For some reason the men who patrolled this wilderness had sought to conceal their living quarters with as much cunning as if they were spies stationed behind enemy lines. Once past the well-hidden doorway, Troy found himself in a large room that served as general living quarters, though screened alcoves along the back wall served for bunk rooms.

There was no heating unit. But a broad platform of stone with an upper opening in the rock roof supported smouldering wood, wood that gave off a spicy, aromatic fragrance as it was eaten into ashes. A flooring of wooden planks had been fitted over the rock beneath their boots, and here and there lay shaggy pelts to serve as small rugs while on the walls were shelves holding not only the familiar boxes of reading tapes, but bits of gleaming rock, some small carvings. Brilliant birdskins had been pieced together in an intricate patchwork pattern to cover six feet of the opposite wall.

It was very far removed from Tikil and the ways of Tikil. But in Troy old memories stirred again. The homestead on Norden had not been quite so rugged, but it had been constructed of wood and stone by men who relied more upon their own strength and skill of hands than upon the products of machines.

The fussel called and was answered from one of the alcoves—not in its own cry, but with a similar note. Troy's other hand shot out to imprison the legs of the hawk before it could fly. But the fussel, stretching out its red-patched neck, its black crest quivering erect, merely uttered a deeper, rasping inquiry. Rerne strode forward, pushed aside the screen. There were three perches in the alcove, one occupied by a bird very different from the one Troy bore.

Where the fussel was sunlit fire, this was a drifting shadow of smoke. Its round head was crestless, but the tufted ears stood erect, well above the downy, haze-gray covering on the skull. Its eyes were unusually large and in the subdued light showed dark as if all pupil. In body it was as large as the fussel, its powerful taloned claws proclaiming it a hunter, as did the tearing curve of its beak.

Now it watched the fussel steadily, but showed only interest, no antagonism. One of the foresters presented a gloved wrist, and it made a bounding leap to that new perch.

"An owhee," Rerne said. "They will willingly share quarters with a fussel."

Troy had heard of the peerless night-hunters but had not seen one before. He watched the ranger take it to the door of the lodge and give it a gentle toss to wing away in the twilight. And a moment later they heard its hunting call: "OOOooowheeee!"

Rerne nodded at the perches and Troy went to let

the fussel make a choice. After a moment of inspection, the bird put claw on the end one and settled there, waiting for Troy to offer him his evening bait.

He who flew the owhee and his partner of the resident staff did not linger after Rerne, Troy, and their kit were in the lodge house. Each forest ranger had a length of trail to patrol by night as well as by day. They said very little, and Troy suspected that it was his presence that kept the conversation to reports, questions, and answers. He tended the fussel and tried to keep out of the way.

But when both had gone and Rerne brought out a pack of Quik-rations, they settled by the fire, which the Hunter poked into renewed life. There were no chairs, only wide, thick cushions of hide stuffed with something that gave forth a pleasant herbal smell when crushed beneath one's weight.

As they shared the contents of the food pack, the Hunter talked and Troy listened. This was the stuff of the other's days—the study of the Wild, the policing of it after a fashion, not to interfere with nature, only to aid her where and when they could, to make sure that the natural destruction wrought by man himself wherever and whenever he came into new territory did not upset delicate ecological balances.

There were stands of fabulous woods that could be cut—but only under the supervision of the Hunting Clans. There were herbs to be sought for the healing fraternities of other worlds, studies made of the native animals. The Wild was a storehouse to which the Clans held the keys—keeping them by force if necessary.

In the tree-filled valleys, on the spreading plains yet farther to the east, battles had been fought between poachers and guardians. And only because Korwar had been proclaimed a pleasure planet did the Clans have the backing to keep the looters out. Most of this Troy knew, vaguely, but now Rerne spoke of times and places, named names.

The story was absorbing, but Troy was no child to be beguiled by stories. He began to wonder at the reason for Rerne's talkativeness.

"There is no carbite on Korwar," Rerne continued. "But let its equal be found here—and let the barriers against mineral exploration go down—"

"Is there any chance of that happening?" Troy ventured, suddenly aware that he, too, was now thinking as a partisan, ready to protect the Wild against willful destruction. Something in him was stirring sluggishly, pressing bonds he himself had welded into place as a self-protection. Like the hawk, he wanted to test his wings against a free and open sky.

Rerne's lips twisted wryly. "We have learned very little, most of our species. I can name you half a hundred planets that have been wrecked by greed. No, not just those burned off during the war, but killed deliberately over a period of years. As long as we can keep Korwar as a pleasant haven for the overlords of other worlds, some of them the greed-wrecked ones, we can hold this one inviolate. One does not want such desolation in one's own back yard. So far those of the villas have the power, the wealth, to retain Korwar as their unspoiled play place. But how long will it continue to be so? There may be other treasures here than those fabled to lie in Ruhkarv, and far more easily found!"

"You have had two hundred years," Troy said, with

71

an old bitterness darkening that elation of moments earlier. "Norden had less than a hundred—thanks to Sattor Commander Di!"

"No length of years will satisfy a man when he sees the end of a way of life he is willing to fight for. What does the past matter when the future swoops for the kill? Yes, Sattor Commander Di—who died of poison in his own garden house and whose murderer is yet to be found—and even the method by which the poison reached him determined—has to answer for Norden."

How did Rerne know all that about Di? The fact of poison had not been broadcast on the general coms. Troy felt like a sofaru rat over which the shadow of a diving fussel had fallen, powerless before the strike of an enemy not of his own element. Was *this* behind Rerne's talk, merely a softening-up process to prepare him for subtle questioning about the kinkajou? Or was his own half-guilty feeling suggesting that?

But the Hunter did not enlarge upon the case of Sattor Commander Di. His explorations into the past were not so immediate. Rather now he led Troy to talk about his own childhood. Though in another Korwarian Horan might have considered that questioning presumptuous, there was something about Rerne's interest that seemed genuine, so that the younger man answered truthfully instead of with the evasions he had used so long for a shield—including the fact that his memories of Norden's plains and the free life there were hazy now.

"There are plains here, too. You might consider that," Rerne suggested cryptically as he arose in one lithe movement. "Given time, the right man might learn much. The bunk at that end is yours, Horan. No

72

evil dreams ride your night—" Again the phrase had some of the formality of a ritual dismissal. Troy looked in upon the fussel, saw that it was asleep with one foot drawn up into its under feathers after the manner of its kind, and then went to the bunk Rerne had indicated.

There was no foam plast filling its box shape. Inside dried grasses and leaves gave under him, then remolded about his body, and the fine scent of them filled his nostrils as he fell asleep easily. He did not dream at all.

When he awoke, the door of the big room stood ajar and from that direction he heard the calls of birds. Still rubbing sleep from his eyes, Troy rolled out of the bunk. The fire on the hearth was out and there was no one else in the room. But the clean smell of a new day in the Wild drew him out on the ledge, to stand looking down into the valley of the lake.

Something rose and fell with a regular stroke not far from the shore, and he realized he was watching a swimmer. A series of steps cut in the rock led down from the ledge, and Troy followed them. Then a loose sleeping robe draped over a bush beckoned him on and he shed his own in turn, testing the temperature of the water with his toes, plunging into it in a clumsy dive before he could change his mind because of that chill greeting.

Troy floundered along the shore, being no expert as was that other now heading, with clean arm sweeps and effortless kicks, back from the center. His threshings disturbed mats of floating blossoms shed by trees bordering a rill that fed the lake at this point, and the bruised petals patterned his wet skin as he found sandy footing and stood up, shivering.

"Storm-cold, Gentle Homo." he commented as Rerne waded in.

The other stopped to wring water from his braided hair knot and then, surveying Troy's dappled body, he laughed.

"A new refinement—flower baths?"

Troy echoed that laugh as he skimmed the wet masses from him. "Not of my choice, Gentle Homo."

"The name is Rerne. We do not follow the paths of Tikil here, Horan." The other was using his nightrobe as a towel, kicking his feet into sandals. With the robe now draped cloakwise about him, he stood for a moment looking out over the lake, and his face was oddly relaxed, much more alive than Troy had ever seen it.

"A fair day. We shall go to the plateau above Stansill and see just how good our feathered one really is."

The flitter took them east and north again. And once more the vegetation beneath them thinned. But not to a waste scar such as that which held Ruhkarv, rather to open plains of tall grasses and scattered, low-growing shrubs. Twice Rerne buzzed the flyer above herds of ruminants, and horned heads tossed angrily before the heavy-shouldered beasts pounded away, tasseled tails high in wrath.

"Pansta," Rerne identified them. "Wild cattle of a sort."

"But they are scaled—or at least they look so!" Troy protested, thinking of his own lost tupan that had grazed so and might have run from a buzzing flitter in the same pattern.

"Not scaled as a fish or a reptile," Rerne corrected. "Those are plates of hardened flesh—something like an insect's wingcasing shell. The herds are dwindling
74

every year, fewer calves born; we do not yet know why. We have reason to believe that they were once domesticated."

"By those of Ruhkarv?"

"Perhaps. Though who or what those of Ruhkarv were—" Rerne shrugged.

"Did they leave only one ruin behind them? I know only of Ruhkarv."

"And that is another mystery. Why a single known city for a civilization? Were they only an outpost of some long-lost stellar empire vanished before man took to space? That was one theory Fauklow wanted to prove or disprove. There is one other trace of them on Korwar—north beyond the plains. But that is all—and that is a very small post. I do not think they were native here. Just as the pansta are so alien to the other animals of the Wild that they do not seem to be native either. The feral herds of a long-gone race, which have outlasted their unknown masters."

The edge of the plains where the pansta ran dropped behind them, and now there were ridges and rising slopes once again, until the flitter climbed to a tableland open to the sky, seeming otherwise cut off from any contact with the lower stretches. Under the golden light of a perfect morning there spread a patched flooring of flowering grasses, a few scattered trees, so removed from any touch of man's passing that Troy thought they might have been the first to find that place if his companion's knowledge of it had not argued otherwise.

Rerne brought the flitter down on a stretch of gravel beside quiet water that was neither as large as a lake nor as small as a pond. They climbed out and stood

75

with the breeze pushing against their bodies. The fussel spread wings, gave voice.

"Let him hunt! Ollllahuuuu!"

Troy gave the wrist flex that was a signal of freedom to the bird he bore. And the fussel arose in great sweeps, beating into the topaz sky until neither man could see him clearly.

Seven

The sun was hot, and from under and around Troy as he lay, the smell of the grass flowers and the grass itself was heady in his nostrils, long pinched by the town and the Dipple. He was relaxed, drowsy, yet not ready to sleep.

It had been a wonderful morning on this piece of Korwar raised into the skies and kept inviolate. Now even the fussel had had enough of the freedom of the wind and the clouds and was content to perch on a tree limb Troy had trimmed and set in the ground for the bird's comfort.

Here the insects seemed few or innocuous. There was no stinging or biting to plague the would-be sleeper. Yet a part of Troy argued that this was very fleeting and that it was a pity to waste a moment in such sloth.

He levered himself up from the warmth. Avoiding the fussel's perch and Rerne's chosen couch, he walked out alone into the open, away from the flitter and all intrusions of Tikil. And as he stood there, the wind trying in vain to pull at his close-cropped hair, pushing protestingly against his straight body, Troy suddenly had a mental picture of a far different place—an artificially lighted room ranked with cages, and the brown-furred back of a creature that had curled into a ball to escape.

The cats—the kinkajou— Here was the fussel, intelligent after its kind—to be trained as another, if beloved, tool or weapon for the use of man. But the Terran creatures—there was a difference, as if somehow they had taken a huge step forward to close ranks with man himself. And Troy knew a tiny flame of excitement. What if that were true? The new world it would open!

He glanced back at Rerne, more than half tempted now to share with the Hunter what was hardly a definite secret—more a series of guesses and surmises. Somehow he thought that in Rerne he would find a believer. Nowhere else on Korwar had he met another with whom he dared be himself, Troy Horan—not a Dippleman, but a free equal. Ever since they had entered the Wild together, this sense of being alive and real again—not aloof from his fellows, but entering once more into a pattern that made for security and solidity—had been growing in him. Now Troy moved slowly, still wary of the wisdom of his half-made decision, but drawn to it. He turned toward Rerne—too late, for the sky was no longer an unoccupied arch of gold. There was a second flitter descending at a speed and angle of approach that suggested urgency.

Rerne sat up in his grassy nest, instantly alert and

ready for action. The flyer touched earth not far from their own flitter. The man swinging out of its cabin wore not the tanned-hide uniform of a ranger on duty, but the more elaborate kilt and tunic of a city dweller. He spoke hastily to the Hunter, and then Rerne beckoned Troy to join them.

"Harse will fly you back to Tikil," he said abruptly, making no explanation for the change of plan. "Tell Kyger that I want the fussel. I will call for it later." He paused, his gaze lingering for a second or two on Troy, almost as if he wanted to add something to that rather curt dismissal. But then he turned away, without any other farewell, climbing into his own flitter.

Troy, chilled, shut out again, a little angry at his own thoughts of only a few moments before, took the fussel on his wrist and joined Harse in the second flyer. Rerne's ship took off in a steep climb and continued north—toward the Clan holdings.

Harse chose the shortest lane back to Tikil. It was late afternoon when, after steady flight, Troy once more entered Kyger's shop. The merchant met him in the courtyard corridor.

"Hunter Rerne?" The ex-spacer looked beyond Troy in search of the other.

Troy explained. Kyger heard him out, his fingers tracing the scar on his cheek as he listened. And it seemed to the younger man that the merchant was waiting to hear something of greater importance than just the confirmation of the fussel's sale.

"Cage it then," Kyger ordered. "And you are in time to help with the last feeding. Get to it!"

One of the yardmen was busy with the water pans in the animal room, but he did not look up as Troy

78

went down the line of cages to that which had held the kinkajou. Only this time there was no round ball of fur in its corner. Another quite different creature, pointed-nosed, sharp-eyed, gazed back at him.

"Back, eh?" The yardman lounged over to lean against the wall. " 'Bout time you got to it, Dippleman. We have done your work an' ours too, an' we have had 'bout enough of that. How did your ride with one of the lords-high-an'-mighty go?"

"Sold the fussel." Troy made a noncommittal answer. He was more interested in what had happened here. Though one Terran animal had disappeared during his absence from the shop, here was another established in the same cage, for he was sure that this newcomer was the beast Kyger had shown to the Grand Leader One, via tri-dee, as a fox.

One Terran animal—no, two! He saw the second one now, curled up much as the kinkajou had been, its back to the world, in the far part of the cage. And he noted that the eyes of the one on guard were as searching in their inspection of him as had been the eyes of the cats. The one on guard—why had he thought that?

"One guards—one sleeps—"

Out of nowhere had come the answer. The fox seated himself now, much as the cats had done in their traveling cage, no longer so wary, more as if ready for some answering move on Troy's part.

"New—what are they?" Troy appealed to the yardman merely to cover his interest in the occupants of the cage.

"Extra-special. And you do not take care of these, Dippleman. Boss's orders. He takes care of them himself."

"Horan!"

Hoping he was able to disguise his somewhat guilty start, Troy glanced back to see Kyger standing at the door of the cage room beckoning.

"Get over here and help Jingu." He shepherded Troy into the tank room where the marine creatures were on display.

On the table at the far end of the room stood a traveling container into which Jingu, the attendant of those particular wares, was measuring a quantity of liquid with an oily sheen to it. A small aquarium containing the same liquid stood before him. And plastered against the side of that was something Troy, at first sight, could not believe existed outside the imagination of some V-dee fantasy creator.

He had seen many weird life forms, either in the flesh or in Kyger's range of tri-dees. But this was not strange; it was impossible—impossible with a kind of stomach-turning horror. He did not want to look at it and yet his eyes were continually drawn back to the aquarium, and, when the thing moved, he fought an answering heave to his stomach.

Leaning against the end of the table, intent upon Jingu's task, was a stranger, a small man wearing the tunic of one of the minor administrative bureaus. He was a colorless man whom one might not have noted or remembered unless seen as he was now, both hands set on the table top as if to lever his slack-muscled body closer to the monster in the aquarium, his eyes avid with—Troy realized—greed, his pale tongue moving back and forth like a lizard's over pale lips. He turned his head as they came up and his eyes were bright.

"Beautiful, Merchant Kyger, beautiful!"

80

Kyger regarded the aquarium occupant bleakly. "Not to me, Citizen. Those hur-hurs are"—he shook his head as might a man at a loss for a descriptive word pungent enough, and then ended rather mildly—"hardly considered beautiful, Citizen Dragur."

The small man might have been the fussel lifting its wings, ready to dart head foward in a beak-sharp attack. "They are a rarity, Merchant Kyger, and of their kind beautiful!" He bristled. "A splendid addition to my collection." He looked from Kyger to Troy. "This young man is to aid in the transporting? I trust that he knows how to handle such valuables safely? I shall hold you responsible, Kyger, until this magnificent specimen is safely installed in my pond room."

Troy opened his mouth to deny that he was going to have any part in the transportation of the hur-hur. Then he caught Kyger's glare and remembered that the seven-day contract was close to renewal time. After all, the carrying jug, or bucket, or whatever they termed it, which Jingu was filling so carefully, did have solid sides, and a cover was waiting to be placed on it. If he did lug the thing around, he did not have to continue to look at it.

Jingu now took up a rod and inserted it carefully, a few inches at a time, beneath the surface of the water in the aquarium. Then he prodded the hur-hur gently. Troy, unable to look away, watched with fascinated disgust as the monster embraced the rod with its profusion of thread-thin tentacles, planting the suckers beading those same tentacles fast on the rod. Then Jingu whipped the rod and hur-hur out of the aquarium into the container and clapped on the lid, adjusting a carrying strap.

Troy lifted the cylinder gingerly, felt it quiver between his hands as apparently the hur-hur chose to resent its new prison with some spirited movements. His fingers shrank from even that contact with the thing inside.

"Be careful!" Dragur shuffled along beside him as he steadied the strap across his shoulder. But Kyger came to his employee's rescue.

"They are not as fragile as all that, Citizen. And here are your obaws for feeding.

He almost thrust a small cage into his customer's hold. The small animals inside were running madly about, squeaking wildly as if they had foreknowledge of their dismal future. Troy, knowing just what that future was in connection with the hur-hur, fought another sharp skirmish with his stomach.

His task was not just to carry the container as far as the flitter awaiting Citizen Dragur, Troy discovered, but to accompany the patron to his home, insuring the safety of the hur-hur while Dragur himself piloted the flyer, at a pace hardly faster than a brisk walk on the ground. Dragur, unlike Rerne, proved to be a babbler. Not that much of his conversation was directed to Horan. Instead, the words that flowed were thoughts uttered aloud and mainly concerned with his now present ability to confound some fellow collector by the name of Supervisor Mazeli, who might outrank Dragur in the hierarchy of the department in which they were both incarcerated until they reached age-for-ease pay, but whose ambitious collection of marine life did *not* embrace a hur-hur.

"Beautiful!" Dragur crawled the flitter across an intersection of avenues, turned into the slightly wider one that led to the outskirts of Tikil. "He will never believe it—never! Next Fellowsday I shall invite him and, say, Wilvins and Sorker. And then I shall escort him around the room, show him the Lupan snails, and the throwworms, give him a chance to enlarge on what *he* has—then—" Dragur lifted one hand from the controls, reached out to pat the top of the container now riding on Troy's knees. "Then—the hur-hur! He will never, never be able to match it. Never!"

For the first time the small man seemed to recollect he did have a human companion in the flitter. "That is correct, is it not, young man? When Merchant Kyger gives a certificate of one-of-a-kind, he does not import during the lifetime of the first specimen? That is truly correct?"

Troy had not heard of that arrangement, but prudence dictated a reply in the affirmative. "I believe so, Citizen."

"Then Mazeli will never have a hur-hur—never! Their life span is two hundred years—maybe three— and Kyger has certified that this is a young one. Oh, Mazeli may wish but he cannot have! Not one such as you, my little beauty!" Dragur delivered another pat to the top of the cylinder. And perhaps some of this elation did register on the monstrosity inside, for the thing gave such a determined lurch against one side that Troy had to hold it steady with both hands.

"Careful! Careful! I say, young man! What are you doing?" Dragur brought the flitter to a complete stop and fronted Troy indignantly.

"I think it is excited, Citizen." Troy held the quivering container with both hands. "It probably wants back in an aquarium."

"Yes, of course." This time Dragur started the flitter with a jerk, and his rate of speed increased appreciably. "We shall soon be there, very soon now—"

Dragur had one of the small share-houses along the merchant zone. He unsealed the palm lock of the door with one hand, waved Troy in with the other. But the atmosphere that met Horan upon entrance was anything but enticing.

There were strange smells to be met in plenty at Kyger's, but a clever system of ventilation and deodorization kept the air from anything but a suggestion of the wares to be offered under that roof. Here the marine reek of the fish room at the shop was multiplied a thousand times.

What had been intended as the meeting room of the share-house was now a miniature sea bottom. The light itself was subdued, in a manner greenish, when compared to the daylight entering through specially tinted panels. And aquariums were set along the walls in banks with what might be a naturally formed pool in the center.

"Stand where you are, right where you are, young man!" Dragur pushed ahead, skirted the floor pool, and approached a table in the darkest corner of that dim chamber. He pulled and pushed at an empty aquarium there until he had it in line with its fellows and then proceeded to lift, with every appearance of exertion, a series of glass containers, pouring from first one and then the other, now and then leaning well over to sniff loudly and rather dramatically at the mixture.

Troy shifted his feet. The weight of the container was not light, and it kept jerking on the shoulder strap as the hur-hur continued to resent transportation. Horan was eager to be out of this cave of bad smells and marine monsters, for some of the things that bumped sides of bowls and aquariums to stare at him, or seem to stare at him, were not far removed from the hur-hur in general frightfulness.

At last the concoction appeared to satisfy Dragur. He added, with the air of an artist supplying the last touch to a masterpiece, a long string of what looked like badly decayed root fibers and beckoned to Troy.

Did Dragur think that *he* was going to transfer the hur-hur via the rod method Jingu had used? If so, this customer was not going to be a satisfied one. Troy had no intention of trying such action.

But apparently Dragur had no idea of leaving such a delicate task to a novice. He waved Troy away again as soon as the other had put down the container and took off the lid. Playing the hur-hur into clinging once more to the rod, the little man whipped the creature with even more dexterity than Jingu had displayed into its new home.

"Now!" Dragur gave the shop container back to Troy. "We must let it alone, strictly alone, two days—maybe three—only visiting it for feeding."

Troy wondered if the other imagined that he was going to be in this smelly room for another few moments, let alone two or three days!

"Is that all, Citizen?" He asked firmly.

Dragur again seemed to notice him as a person. "What? Ha—yes, that will be all, young man. I have not seen you before, have I? You did not come with me last time for a delivery."

"No. I am new at Kyger's."

"Yes, it was Zul who came last time, I remember. And who are you, young man?"

"Troy Horan."

"Horan? Horan—that is an off-world name, surely?"

"I am from Norden," Troy returned as he edged toward the outer door with its promise of fresh air.

"Norden?" Dragur blinked as if trying to visualize some solar chart on which he could place Norden with dispatch and precision. "You are a former spacer then, as is Merchant Kyger?"

"I am from the Dipple."

"Oh." Dragur displayed the conventional citizen's reaction to that, embarrassment intermixed with irritation. "Assure Merchant Kyger that I am pleased, very pleased. I shall be in myself, of course, with my supply list. And please remind him that this is a one-of-a-species sale—that must be plain, very plain."

"I am sure the merchant understands, Citizen."

Dragur followed him to the door, pointed out the nearest roll walk. He did not reenter the house until Troy was several paces away. Probably, thought Horan bitterly, he just wants to make sure a Dippleman is well off the premises.

But this was not the end of a day of minor irritations and disappointments. The morning had begun so well with the awakening in the lodge of the Wild. It was ending in the evening in Tikil with his re-entering the shop to discover Zul very much the master of the cage room. Though the small yellow man walked with a limp, he walked briskly, and he did not welcome Troy back.

End of the seven-day contract—Troy was very conscious of that. He could continue here to the limit of that time and then Kyger was under no obligation to renew. With Zul back he probably would not. When Troy brought in water for the fox cage, the other waved him off, attending to the Terran animals himself. In fact he zealously preempted so many of the tasks Troy had done that the latter was elbowed out of the work almost entirely. And each time Horan saw Kyger he expected to be told that his employment would be over as soon as it was legally possible to dismiss him.

However, the merchant said nothing—until a few moments immediately preceding the official closing of the shop. Then Troy was summoned to where Kyger and Zul stood by the door of the animal room. And he could see that Zul was not pleased.

"You will take the night inspection tours as usual," Kyger ordered. His broad fingers rested on Zul's shoulder, and now he pulled the smaller man with him as easily as if Zul were powerless in his hold. The yellow man favored Troy with a glare that made the latter wish, not for the first time, that he had a right to wear a belt knife.

With the shop closed and the animals settled, Troy made his first round, starting with the now silent customer's lounges, checking each room. What he was hunting, or why he had this growing compulsion that was almost a search, he could not have told.

The lounges contained nothing out of the ordinary; the bird room was as always. He lingered before the fussel. It was hard to remember this morning. The bird permitted him to run a forefinger along its crest, drew the bill that could stab and kill across his hand in return.

Then he was in the animal room. And now he thought

he knew what had driven him to this restless seeking. What *had* become of the kinkajou? No one had mentioned it since his return. The foxes had been settled in its place as if they had been there for days. Had it been returned to the Sattor Commander Di's heirs as a valuable part of his estate?

Suddenly Troy knew that he would have to discover what had become of the animal that had claimed his aid and that he might have unknowingly left unprotected, for he remembered all too well the strange conversation in the night.

On impulse he turned and left the cage room, walked straight to his bunk and stretched out on it. If he could not find the kinkajou one way, there was a chance—just a very faint chance—another and more devious path might serve.

Eight

Troy's eyes were shut. He willed nerves and muscles to relax, trying to hit by chance, since he had no better guide, on the pattern that had aided him that other night to tune in upon the exchange that was not conversation. Through the coms all the usual noises from the bird and animal rooms reached him, and he tried not to listen.

"—here. Out—"

Not really words, rather impressions—a signal, a

plea. Troy's eyes opened; he sat up—and that whisper of contact was gone. Angry at his own lack of control, he settled himself once more on the bunk, tried again to tap that band of communication.

"Out—out—danger—"

He lay, hardly breathing, trying to hold that line.

"Out—"

Yes, it was a plea; he was certain of that. But there was no way of discovering from whom or from where it came. He might have stumbled upon a small loop of rope in the middle of a large room, to be told to find the coil from which it had been cut.

"Where?" He tried to frame that word in his own mind, force the inquiry into the band he could not locate.

Then he received an impression of surprise—so strong it was like an exclamation his ears could pick up.

"Who? Who?" The query was eager, demanding.

"Troy—" He thought his own name but was answered by a sense of bafflement, disappointment. Maybe names meant nothing in this eerie exchange. Troy tried to build up a mental picture of his own face as he had seen it in mirrors. He thought intensely of that face, of each detail of his own features.

The sensation of bafflement faded, though he was sure he had not lost contact.

"Who?" he asked silently in return, certain that he was communicating with the kinkajou.

But instead an oddly shaped and distorted picture of a triangular mask, sharp-pointed nose, glittering eyes, pricked ears—the fox!

Troy slipped out of his bunk. He did not foresee any trouble. If Kyger or Zul turned up, he could always say he was investigating some unusual sound. Yet he took the stunner from its wall niche before he left the small room and went as noiselessly as he could down the corridor to the animal room.

There was a cover over the front of the fox cage. Troy raised that flap. Both animals sat there, watching him. He glanced about the room. Even in the dim night light he could see nothing amiss. This could not be a case of an intruder as it had been when the kinkajou's warning had saved his life.

"What is wrong?" At the moment there was nothing strange in his standing there thinking that question at a pair of Terran foxes.

"The big one—he threatens."

It was as if someone with a strictly curtailed number of words was trying to convey a complex thought. The big one—Kyger?

"Yes!" The assent was quick, eager.

"What is wrong?"

"He fears—thinks better dead—"

"Who is better dead?" Troy's grip on the stunner tightened. He felt a cold stab between his shoulders giving birth to a chill that had nothing to do with the temperature of the room.

"Those who know—all those who know—"

"Me?" Troy countered quickly. Though of what Kyger might suspect him or why he had no idea.

There was no answer. Either he had presented them with a new puzzle, or, unable to give a definite reply, they gave none at all.

"You?"

"Yes—" But there was an element of doubt in that yes.

"Others like you?" Troy pushed.

"Yes!" Now there was no mistaking the vehemence of that.

He thought of the kinkajou. One of the foxes reared, put front paws against the screening of the cage. "It was here. Now it is there."

"Where?" Troy tried to follow.

His mind pictured for him a cage, hooded and stored—but not in any room of the shop he had seen.

"In the yard pens?" he asked.

There was a long moment before the answer came and then it was evasive.

"Cool air, many smells—maybe outside."

Was the fox only relaying for the kinkajou? Troy thought that might be true.

"Cage covered—not to see—"

That fitted. The animal might well be in one of the outside pens still in a carrying cage. But to find it tonight would be a risky project, and what could he do if he did locate it?

"Hide!"

They had picked that out of his thoughts, replied to it. The standing fox was panting a little, its red tongue lolling from its jaws.

Troy considered the problem. For some reason Kyger had hidden the kinkajou, intending to get rid of it. To meddle in this at all was simply asking for trouble. Not only would the merchant break contract, but he was entitled to black-list Troy with the C.L.C. so that he could never hope for another day's labor on Korwar. That had happened to Dipplemen in the past, and for less cause. He had only to fasten down the cover of the foxes' cage, leave the room, forget everything, and he was safe.

How safe? He stared down at the fox. The kinkajou, the foxes, even the cats, all knew that he was able to communicate with them. Suppose they passed the information on to Kyger? That interrupted conversation the other night—if Kyger knew he had "heard" that— Yes, a refusal to help might cut two ways now.

He jerked the flap of the cage cover into place, making no further attempt to talk to the foxes. Then, thrusting the stunner into the top of his rider's belt, he padded to the rear door and let himself out cautiously, ducking into a convenient pool of shadow.

Just as he patrolled the shop during the night, the senior yardman made the rounds out here. And Troy's presence near some of the larger animal pens could arouse their inhabitants to noisy protest, betraying him at once. Nor did Horan have the least idea in which of these enclosures the kinkajou was now housed, if it was here at all.

He slipped along the wall, his left shoulder against it, making a quick dart across an open space to the shelter of a doorway. From that came the scent of hay, seeds, dried vegetation. And those mingled odors took him back to his twenty-four hours in the Wild. Perhaps it was then that the first flick of an idea was born—not concrete enough yet to be called a plan, just a hazy half-dream suggesting a way of escape if Kyger did dismiss him again to the Dipple.

Troy felt the door yield to his gentle push and he went in. Under his hand the panel swung almost closed once more, but through the crack he was able to reconnoiter the rest of the courtyard. In which of the pens and cages about its circumference could what he sought be effectively hidden? And would Kyger have undertaken that mission himself or left it to one of the yardmen—or Zul?

Kyger—or Zul, the most likely. Zul had not wanted Troy to be left in the shop tonight; he was certain of that. He wished he knew where that small man was right now.

There was a stir by the door that gave on the passage leading to Kyger's private apartment. A figure moved into the open and Troy saw Zul, by his present actions a Zul who did not want to be observed, for, as Troy had done, the other took advantage of every shadow to cover his journey along the row of pens.

Perhaps the creatures penned there were used to his scent and such nighttime journeys, for none of them roused. Then Zul disappeared, seemingly into a patch of wall. Where his flitting had been soundless, the tap of footsteps now sounded briskly down the opposite side of the yard, and Troy held his breath as they approached the supply room. He gently eased the panel fully shut and waited tensely to see if the patrolling guard would try it.

When the footfalls passed without pausing, Horan again opened the door a crack. He could not see the retreating yardman from this position, but he heard the door at the other end of the court close. Then he saw Zul detach himself from the wall and move on. So—Zul was keeping this a secret from the regular guard? That was most interesting.

Two, three more pens the other passed. Then he stopped before the last in that row, a larger enclosure where two small trasi from Longus were kept. They were very tame and most affectionate creatures of a subspecies of deer.

The pen door opened and Zul disappeared within, the darkness there hiding him entirely.

"Obey!"

Troy's hand went to his head at the force of that menacing thought-order, which struck like a blow. But to it there was not the faintest trace of an answer, either agreement or protest. Somehow Troy could imagine Zul stooped above a shrouded cage, trying to arouse a ball of fur that remained stubbornly impervious to his commands.

"Listen!" Again that whip crack of order. "You will obey!"

Again only complete silence. Will against will— animal opposing man? Troy leaned his forehead against the cool surface of the door behind which he half crouched, trying with every fiber of will and strength to listen in on the duel that he was sure was being waged across the courtyard.

Minutes dragged. Then Zul slid out of the pen, made his way back along the wall, disappeared into the same passage the spacers used when they visited the shop. Troy counted slowly under his breath. When he reached fifty and there was no movement in the courtyard, he came out of the storeroom, went to the trasi pen.

The animals stirred as he lifted the latch and let himself in. Only a little of the limited light in the yard reached here, and at first he thought that he must have been mistaken; there was no cage in sight. He stooped, brushed through the hay piled against the far wall, to bark his knuckles painfully against solid surface. Then he hunkered down, feeling over the covered cage for the fastenings. They had been doubly tied and he had difficulty in loosening them.

Though the kinkajou must have been aware of his efforts, it made no move, neither a stir nor a mind touch. The flap of the cover was up now, but Troy could not see into the cage. He unfastened the catch of the door.

Troy fell back as a half-seen thing flashed into the loose hay, tossing up a small whirlwind of scattered wisps, squeezed under the bottom of the pen door and was gone—before the man half comprehended that the captive had been poised ready for escape. There was no use now trying to find it in the courtyard. There were a hundred places that might have been designed to conceal a fast-moving arboreal animal such as the kinkajou—which left Troy where?

He snapped shut the cage, refastened the covering the same way he had found it. Brushing hay from his coveralls, he detached a last telltale length from his belt. There was no use in looking for more trouble. The kinkajou was loose, and he could not help believing that the animal was far safer at this moment than it had been in that cage. Let its empty prison provide a morning mystery for Kyger or Zul.

Troy went back to his bunk. He was convinced now that his employer had a part in a game more important than smuggling, a game in which the animals were involved. And as he dozed off, he wondered just how many four-footed Terrans with strange mental powers had been loosed on Korwar—and why.

If the kinkajou had been missed, there was no alarm given the next day. The routine followed the same pattern it had every morning that Troy had been employed by Kyger's, with the exception that Zul now took over a major portion of the indoor work and Troy was relegated to sweeping and cleaning jobs, which were the least desirable. But at noon he was summoned to the bird room, for it appeared that competent as he might be in other ways, Zul was not the handler favored by the fussel.

Troy could hear the bird's angry screams while he was still in the corridor. And Kyger, scowling, stood waving him to hurry. Zul, chattering in some language other than Galbasic, was fairly dancing in his own heat of rage, a bleeding hand held now and again to his wide-lipped mouth as he sucked a deep tear in the flesh.

Troy spoke to the merchant. "We shall have to have quiet."

Kyger nodded, reached out for Zul, and manhandled the struggling man out. The fussel was beating its wings, its beak stretched to the limit as it screamed.

Troy approached the bird slowly, crooning a monotone of such small soothing sounds as, he had discovered during his night rounds, combatted the suspicions and alarms of any disturbed cage dweller. There was no hurrying this. To arouse the fussel to the state of fighting against the cage would be to damage the bird, if not physically, then emotionally. Troy summoned all his concentration of mind and body, unconsciously trying to reach the bird's mind by the same method he had used to communicate with the Terran animals. He was aware of no response in return, but the fussel did quiet, until, at last, Troy could take it out on his wrist. He moved to the door, eager to walk the bird in the open where it might lose its agitation.

Kyger stood aside for him. "The courtyard," he suggested. "I will see you have it free for a space."

An hour later the great hawk was restored to good humor and Troy returned it to the cage. He was pulling off his glove when Kyger joined him.

"That was well done. We can use you on staff. Will you take full contract?"

This was what he had hardly dared hope for—a contract that would register him as a subcitizen! He would be free of the Dipple forever, since you were not demoted from a full contract except for a very serious criminal cause; the laws of Korwar would operate in his favor, not against him, from now on. Yet—there were all those nagging little doubts, and the affair of the kinkajou. Beneath that was something else as well, the feeling that he did not want to be a loyal employee of Kyger's, tied by custom and ethics to the purposes of the shop. What he did want he had sensed only vaguely that morning on the plateau in the Wild—a freedom not to be found in Tikil. But that was stupid. Troy disciplined his wishes never to be realized and looked to his employer with all the gratitude he could muster.

"Yes, Merchant, I accept."

"Another day for the old contract to run—then the new. Meanwhile"—Kyger observed the fussel—"we don't want any more trouble with this one. I will com the Hunter Headquarters in the city and if they will accept delivery on Rerne's behalf, you can take the bird there tonight."

But within the hour Zul brought a message from Kyger, and Troy came to the office to find the merchant striding up and down, his fingers picking at his scar. He had never given the impression of an easily disturbed man, but he was not the calm and confident purveyor of luxuries to Tikil now.

"We close early," he told Troy. "Do not answer any queries on the door com. And make your rounds on time. I will not be here—but if there is any trouble, hit the alarms at once. Do not try to handle it yourself. The patrollers will take over."

What did Kyger expect, an armed invasion? Troy knew that this was not the time to ask anything. The other had gathered up a hooded night cloak—usually the garment for one venturing into the less reputable portions of the town—and he was wearing his service blaster. It was a certain bleak look in his eyes, a set to his jaw, that warned off questions.

To Troy's satisfaction Zul accompanied his master. Now, with the shop closed and yet the hour early, he would have a chance to look about the courtyard. He did not believe that the kinkajou would remain in hiding there unless the fact that it must have imported food would tie it to the source of supply. But maybe he could prove or disprove that theory tonight.

There were only two places that had not been open to constant view during the day—the storeroom in which he had taken refuge the night before and Kyger's own quarters. The latter he had no hope of exploring. They would be locked, to be opened only by the pressure of the merchant's own hand—or a blaster.

But the storeroom, filled with boxes, bales, containers, had a score of hiding places into which a frightened animal could tuck itself. The foxes in the animal room—the kinkajou free. Troy could not rid himself of the thought that those three might be in contact. Would he be able to reach and influence the fugitive through the two still in the cage? And why were they still in the shop? To Troy's knowledge there had been

98

no message sent to the Grand Leader One that her pets had arrived.

Armed with a food box, he went to the animal room. Again the foxes' prison was curtained. Troy loosened the flap. One of the animals was sleeping, or seeming to sleep. The other also sprawled, its eyes half closed. And seeing them, Troy could almost doubt his belief in their powers.

"Where is the other?" he thought, trying to get into that demand a little of the force Zul had used in his questioning of the kinkajou.

The waking fox yawned, then brought its jaws together with a snap, its eyes still bemused—with no outward interest in Troy at all. The man tried again, throttling down his impatience, using the same gentle approach he had brought to the soothing of the fussel—with no result. If there was any contact between the foxes and the fugitive, they would not employ it for Troy. He would have to hunt on his own.

He was on his way back to the courtyard when the com shrilled, drawing him to the nearest viewplate. The clouded image there settled into a rather fuzzy focus of Kyger's features.

"Horan?"

Troy thumbed the answer lever. "Here, Merchant."

"You will turn guard duty over to Jingu and deliver the fussel to the Hunter Headquarters in the Torrent District. Understand?"

"Understood," Troy assented. There went his hopes for exploring the storeroom. He went to tidy his clothes, and then to select a traveling cage for the bird. Would Rerne be there, back from his mysterious errand? He found himself hoping so.

Nine

Tikil at night, or at least during the early hours of the night, was more crowded than by day. Horan called an accommodation flitter for his crosstown journey to the Hunter Headquarters, but he decided to use the roll walk on his return. He was going toward it when Harse hailed him, just in front of the building.

"You seek Rerne?"

"I brought the fussel, by Merchant Kyger's orders." Troy was put on the defensive by the other's attitude. During their brief time together Rerne had never made him conscious of the Dipple. With the other rangers Horan was ever aware of his knifeless belt and the fact he was a planetless man.

"There is a message," Harse replied aloofly. "Rerne wishes to speak with you—"

"But I was just told he is not here."

"So he is elsewhere. Come!"

Troy was tempted to reply "no" to that curt order. After all, he was not under contract to Rerne. Yet he could not deny that he was interested to learn why Harse had been sent to find him.

The other was as adept at threading a fast passage through the crowds as he might have been in finding a path through the forests. And he brought Troy not to any office or lounge, but to one of those small eating places that sprang up overnight by public favor and disappeared as quickly when some newer attraction drew the fickle pleasure seekers.

"Fourth booth," Harse said and left him.

Troy pushed his way in and discovered that his shop livery did not make him conspicuous here. This café definitely catered to subcitizens and the lower ranks of shop employees. Two of the booths were curtained, signifying private parties. But there were two men without feminine company in the one to which he had been directed.

Rerne, wearing shop livery, sat with his back against the wall. And with him was an older man in a dark tunic lacking any emblems of rank, yet equipped with that indefinable aura of authority that Troy recognized as the inborn assurance of a man who has held responsibility from his early years.

"Horan—" Rerne uttered his name in what might be a greeting, but more likely was an introduction for the stranger's benefit.

"Rogarkil." Now the stranger nodded to Troy.

"You have taken permanent contract with Kyger?" Rerne shot that question at him bluntly, even as he waved the younger man to a seat.

"I will—tomorrow—" A subtle tone in the other's demand made him uneasy, put him on the defensive—why, he could not have said.

"You are now under a short-term one?" That was Rogarkil.

"That is so."

"And if you should be offered employment elsewhere?"

"I have given my word to Merchant Kyger. He would have to agree to my going."

Rogarkil smiled wryly. "There are always such

disadvantages when one deals with honorable men. And to deal with dishonorable ones is to lose before one takes the first stride in a race. So at this hour you are still Merchant Kyger's man?"

"I am."

What did they want of him? This talk of honor and dishonor made Troy uncomfortable. But Rerne did not give him time to speculate about the meanings that might lie behind their fencing blades of words.

"There are questions you can answer, which will in no way break contract. For example: Is it not true that Merchant Kyger is now in the process of importing a Terran animal known as a fox at the express order of the Great Leader?"

"You yourself heard that order given, Gentle Homo."

"And he has imported other Terran animals?"

"As you say, Gentle Homo, he has imported other Terran animals. This must be general knowledge, since the display of such pets is the pleasure of those who buy them."

"A pair of cats for the Gentle Fem San duk Var, a kinkajou for Sattor Commander Di—"

"I am a cleaner of cages and do general labor for the worthy merchant," Troy returned stiffly. "I do not make sales, nor do I see many of the great ones who buy."

"But among those cages that you clean," cut in Rogarkil, "are doubtless those of some of these exotics You have seen some of them with your own eyes, young man?"

Troy kept strictly to the record. "I was with Subcitizen Zul when he went to the port to accept delivery of the cats—"

"And you met with some trouble that morning—"

Troy looked slowly from one man to the other. "Gentle Homos," he said softly, "if I speak now to patrollers not in uniform, I have the right to know that fact. There is still law to protect a man in Tikil—even one from the Dipple."

Rogarkil grimaced. "Yes, you are entirely within your rights, young man, to deliver such a counterthrust as that. No, we are not patrollers—nor do we represent the law of Tikil. This is a Clan matter. Do you understand what that means?"

"Even in the Dipple, Gentle Homo, men have ears and lips. Yes, I know that the Clans are older than the city law, that they are rumored to have powers even beyond those of the Council Governor-General. But they are of the Clans and for the Clans. I am of the Dipple and if I am to climb out of the Dipple, I must do so under the laws of Tikil. Why you ask me these questions I do not know, but I hold by contract rights. This much I will say—and it is no more than you can learn from the patroller records—I have seen the cats. And I took the kinkajou from the villa of Sattor Commander Di. It had been frightened by rough handling there. I have seen the foxes, which are now in the shop. Why should these facts be of any importance?"

"That is what we are striving to learn," Rogarkil answered enigmatically. "You are right, Horan. Clan law does not run in Tikil. But remember that it does run elsewhere—"

"A threat—or a warning, Gentle Homo?"

"A warning. We have reason to believe that you walk on the rim of a whirlpool, young man. Take good care that you do not leap into its current."

"That is all you have to ask me?"

Rogarkil waved his hand in dismissal. But Rerne arose as Troy did.

"I will see Merchant Kyger."

"Not tonight. The shop is closed."

Both men eyed him now as if he had made some fateful announcement.

"Why?"

"Kyger had an errand—"

Rerne turned to his companion, spoke a sharply accented sentence in a language that was not Galbasic. Rogarkil asked Troy another question: "Is not this foreign to your regular routine?"

"Yes."

"So—well, maybe Merchant Kyger's personal affairs are beginning to press him more acutely," he commented. "One cannot carry a knife in two quarrels and give equal attention to both. But the foxes are still there?" He turned to Troy. "And where is the kinkajou you took from Di's villa—also in the shop?"

Troy shrugged. "When I returned from the Wild, it was gone from the cage room. Perhaps it was restored to the Sattor Commander's heirs. It is a very valuable asset of the estate."

"Kyger did not return it so," Rerne stated with finality. He was watching Troy narrowly now, coldly.

"It was gone from its cage." Troy repeated the part-truth stubbornly. He was not going to add to that when he did not know the game they were playing—the nature of this "whirlpool" in which he, too, could be trapped.

"The boy is right, of course," Rogarkil said. "Employed as casual labor, he would have no reason to know more than he has noticed. And he is a man under contract, apart from our problems. It is a pity this is so now, Horan. Under other circumstances we might have been of mutual assistance to one another. A rider of Norden is not too far removed in aspirations and desires from a Hunter of Korwar."

"There are no riders on Norden today," Troy pointed out. He was watching Rerne, and again it seemed to him that the Hunter was two-minded, about to speak and then thinking better of it. Instead he nodded and Troy took that gesture for one of dismissal. He lifted his own hand in a small salute—one of equality though he was not aware of that—and walked away from the booth. Why was he gnawed by the feeling that he had just slammed a door irrevocably, a door that might have opened on a new world? There was an ache of disappointment in him that was like the bite of an old inappeasable hunger.

He pushed through the crowds, hardly noticing those about him, made his way back to the shop and the side entrance into the courtyard. Slapping his hand against the signal plate, he waited for the night yardman to activate the open beam for him. But instead, at that touch from his open palm, the panel swung inward and he was looking down the short covered way, a way that was unnaturally dim as if the usual night-radiance bars there had been set at least two notches lower than was normal.

Troy's stunner was in the bunk room. He was unarmed, and he had no intention of walking that courtyard without some form of defense. The door had no right to be open; the dimmed lights underlined that silent warning. He could well be facing a trap.

Now he unfastened the polished silver buckles of his

105

belt. The strip of metal-encrusted leather was the onl
thing on him that could serve as a weapon. With on
end grasped tightly in his fist, the length ready to us
as a lash, he edged along the wall of the passage
listening to catch any sound from the courtyard beyond

The mild complaints of the animals penned ther
could cover an attack. But from whom and for wha
purpose? Troy reached the end of the passage, flattene
his body against the wall just inside the entrance, an
surveyed the open. There was something wrong abou
the south side—

Then he pinpointed that difference. The door tha
led to Kyger's private quarters, which he had neve
seen open, stood ajar now—painting an unfamilia
shadow across a section of pavement. And in the cente
of the yard stood a flitter. Whether it was the sho
flyer he could not tell.

The open door and that waiting flyer were not al
There was an atmosphere of sharp expectancy abou
the whole scene—as if the stage awaited actors. Mayb
the animals were sensitive to that also, for there wer
only the most subdued sounds from the pens. Again Tro
smelled "trap" as if it were a tangible odor in the ai
But somehow he could not believe it was set for him

Kyger then? That fitted better. He had had hints
some personal difficulty—perhaps even a knife feud—
engulfing the merchant. And there was the Clan'
concern with the ex-spacer, too. Troy Horan was ver
small fry indeed. This suggested an operation on
much more important scale.

Prudence dictated his getting across that courtyar
into his own bunk room, without any exploration—i
he could make it unobserved by what might hide ou

there. And what about Zul? The little man had left with Kyger—but what if he had returned separately? The yardmen? From what he could see, there was no indication that there was any human anywhere in the store block.

A flicker of movement, not in the courtyard but on the top of one of the blocks of pens, drew Troy's eyes. There was a second such. Something small, dark, fluidly supple, had crossed a patch of light, been followed by another such. Far too small to be Zul—animals loose from some cage? But why on the roof coming *in?* The shadows into which both had slipped were far too deep for his sight to penetrate, and the speed with which they had disappeared suggested they might already be far away from that point.

A gathering—why did he think of that? Troy measured the distance between him and the nearest cover. Then, with as much speed as he could muster, he made that leap, stood listening once more, his breath coming raspingly.

Another surge of shadow, drawn toward that half-open door of Kyger's. This moving, not with the slinking glide of the patch on the roof, but in a quick, scuttling dash, again too hurried for Troy to see clearly. But he was sure it whipped about the edge of the door, went into the merchant's private quarters.

Troy made his own advancing rush. Then he saw round balls of green turned up toward him from close to ground level, feral animal eyes. The belt swung in his hand, his reaction to being so startled. They were gone as another form went through the door.

His earlier alarm had been tinged with curiosity. Now there was another emotion feeding it. Just as those shadows had gone to the waiting door, so did he have to follow. He crossed the last few feet and entered, somehow expecting an attack.

Here the sounds from the courtyard were muted. But there was that which was not a sound, rather a thrumming in the blood, a throb in the ears—less than audible sound, or more. He knew of whistles, animal and bird calls, that sounded notes beyond the human range of hearing. Yet he could feel this that he could not hear, and it was an irritant, a disturbance that nourished fear. But he could not turn his back upon it.

Troy groped his way forward, for there was no night ray on. Then his foot touched a rising surface and he explored a stairway with his hands. Step by step he climbed, the thick substance of the footing soaking up any sound of his boots. The throb was beating more heavily through his body as he went.

The stairway ended. He stood listening—and knew that no longer was he alone, though no sound, not even that of a hurried breath, betrayed whoever, or whatever, shared that darkness with him.

Troy had no idea of the geography of the space in which he now was, and there could not be any open window slits, for the dark was complete. He kept stern rein on his imagination, which tended to people this place with shapes that crept and slunk toward the target—which was himself. On impulse he squatted on his heels, marked off a foot or so on the belt he held, and swung it from left to right at floor level. Sure of that much clear space, he inched on to try the same maneuver again.

How long he might have taken to make the trip

across the hall Troy was never to know, for a sudden shaft of light speared dazzlingly from right to left some feet away. And as his eyes adjusted to that, Troy saw it issued from a panel door not quite closed.

He was in a hallway from which three such doors issued, all of them on his right. And it was the last one that showed the light. No sound—but he could not retreat now. Someone—or something—knew he was there, was waiting. And he had to face it.

On his feet again, Troy moved lightly and swiftly to that panel. His hand touched its surface—now he could look in, though he was not sure the man in that room could see him.

Kyger sat there, not in the enveloping embrace of an eazi-rest, but upright on a queer, backless, armless stool, his shoulders against the wall. And between his hands was a cylinder perhaps a foot in diameter, one end resting on the floor guarded by his firmly planted boots, its top slightly below his chin.

No man could sit that quietly, not if he was conscious. Yet Kyger's eyes were open, staring—not at Troy as the other first supposed, but beyond and through him, as if the younger man had no existence. And that frozen stare moved Troy forward, made him push open the panel and step within.

Kyger did not stir. Troy, tongue running across suddenly dry lips, came on. It was an oddly bare room. There was Kyger on his stool, gripping his cylinder. There was a series of small polished cabinets, all closed and with plainly visible thumb locks, and that was all.

Troy spoke and then wished he had not as his words echoed hollowly. "Merchant Kyger—is there something wrong?"

Kyger continued to stare and Troy at last knew the truth—Kyger was a dead man. He whirled, seeking behind him the one who had put on the light—to see nothing save a wall on which there were patterned lines of red, black, and white laid down in a map's design. A map of Tikil, he realized as he surveyed it, in which the open door panel had left a break in the eastern section.

Purposefully Troy moved to the right of the seated man. He could see no wound, no indication of any violence. Yet Kyger had not died naturally—his position, this room, argued that. And what of the thing or things that he had seen precede him through the downstairs door?

Leaving the panel open for light, Troy went back into the hall, pushed open both other doors. One gave on a bedchamber, the other on a small lounge-diner, both empty.

He went back to Kyger's room. And now, fronting him out of nowhere, were those shadows—the black cat and its blue-gray mate, the kinkajou, no longer an indifferent ball but very much alert, the two foxes he could have sworn were safe in their cage in the other building. It looked as if the full roll of Terran imports to Korwar was before him now. And their lips were drawn back from their teeth, the hair of the cats was roughened on their arched backs, their united menace could be felt as a blow.

"No!" Oddly enough he answered that unvoiced rage and fear with word and gesture, dropping the belt, holding his hands up and palm out to them as if he faced another of his own species.

The black cat relaxed first, pacing forward a paw's

length or so, and Troy dropped on one knee. "No," he repeated as firmly but in a lower tone. Then he held out his hand as he had seen Kyger do on the morning they had first uncrated the cats in the courtyard.

A delicate sniff or two, and then sharp teeth closed on the back of his wrist, not to hurt, he knew, but as if to seal some agreement. Troy did not have a chance to learn more, for there was a sound from below. Someone who had no reason to disguise his coming was climbing the stairs.

Troy strode to the panel of the hall door. Then he knew that his silhouette could be seen from below, and he ducked to one side. It was the action of only a few seconds, but when he glanced at the animals, they were gone. Where they had vanished to he could not guess, but that they had their suspicions concerning the newcomer he could deduce from that disappearance.

There was no such escape for him. Troy stepped back a little, picked up his belt, and, with it ready in his hand, stood waiting.

Zul came into the path of the light. He gave Troy a wide-eyed stare, looked beyond to the motionless Kyger. Then, his lips pulled tight against his teeth, just as the animals had snarled, he launched himself at Troy, his knife out, a vicious streak of fire in his hand.

Ten

Troy dodged and licked out with his belt lash for the wrist of Zul's knife hand. The buckle-loaded tip found its mark, and the smaller man yelped and swung around so that his outflung, balancing arm brushed against the tube Kyger's dead fingers steadied. The cylinder fell and the body of the merchant followed it, wilting bonelessly to the floor. Zul screeched, a cry as high and unhuman as any the animals or birds could have uttered.

At the same time Troy felt a cessation of that thrumming throb. The tube rolled toward him, and Zul, seeming to forget his rage of only seconds earlier, made a grab for it.

Troy kicked, sending the tube spinning. Then he brought the edge of his hand down across Zul's neck, dropping the little man to lie on the floor gasping. Troy had leisure to collect both knife and cylinder before Zul sat up, still breathing in hoarse rasps.

With the knife and tube laid on top of a cabinet, Troy advanced on Zul. It was like trying to master by force a frenzied animal, one that scratched and bit. In spite of his repugnance, Troy was forced to knock the smaller man out in order to fasten his hands behind him with his own belt.

Troy was rebuckling his riders broad cincture when

112

he saw Zul's eyes open and take in the limp body of Kyger. The small man's face twisted in a grimace Troy could not read. Then he strained to raise his head from the floor, looked about eagerly, as if he wanted something more important for the moment than Troy. His attention centered on the tube where it lay with one end projecting over the edge of the cabinet, and he actually began to wriggle his body across the floor toward it.

Troy stepped between. Zul's grimace was now an open snarl. He spat, struggled to lever himself from the floor.

Troy picked up the tube and took it with him as he moved to the red alarm button on the wall. The quicker he summoned the authorities, the less trouble he would have in telling his own tale.

"No!" For the first time Zul spoke intelligibly. "Not the patrollers!"

"Why not? I have nothing to hide. Have you?"

Zul's frantic squirming across the room had brought him to the row of cabinets. Now he wriggled his shoulders up against that support so that he was sitting, not lying.

"No patrollers!" he repeated, and his words now held the tone of an order rather than a plea. "Not yet—"

"Why?"

Zul's dark eyes were again focused on the tube Troy held. He was plainly a man torn between the need for secrecy and the necessity of having help.

Troy pressed. "Because of the animals—the Terran animals?"

Zul froze, his small body suddenly rigid, his face the

113

personified mask of surprise—and perhaps some other emotions Troy could not read.

"What do you know?" His words were harsh, rasping, as if he had to fight for the breath to expel them.

"Enough." Troy hoped that ambiguity would force some revelation out of his captive.

Zul's tongue tip wet his lips. He hitched his shoulders along the cabinets as if to reach Troy.

"They must be killed—quickly—before the patrollers are called."

Troy was startled. Death for those who had met him in this room was the last thing he would have expected from Zul. And certainly he had no intention of yielding to that.

"Why?"

Zul's eyes changed, became sly and suspicious once again. "If you do not know, Dippleman, then you know nothing. They are a danger—to all of us under this roof they are a great danger, now that their master is dead. You will kill, or you will wish that you had died also."

Troy covered the space between them in one long-legged stride. He stooped, caught Zul by the collar of his tunic, and pulled him to his feet, holding him pinned against a cabinet.

"You will tell me why these animals are a danger," he said softly, trying to put into that speech all the force and menace he could muster.

"Because"—Zul's eyes were lifted to Troy's; apparently he was making a last throw, which might or might not contain the truth—"they are more than animals. They think, they take orders, they report—"

"What orders do they take, and to whom do they report?"

114

Zul swallowed visibly. There were small beads of oily moisture forming on his forehead just below the tight knots of his hair. Yet Troy sensed that he was not afraid of his captor, but of something else. "They take their orders from him who summons them." Zul's eyes flicked to the tube and back again to Troy's face. "And they report to him—"

"What?"

"Information."

Puzzle pieces clicked together in Troy's mind. Pets—with the ability to understand their masters' or mistresses' actions, to collect information—planted in households where information worth a high price could be gathered!

"And Kyger did this?" That was a statement as well as a question.

"Yes. Now the animals must be summoned and killed before the patrollers arrive. Give me the caller."

"I think not." So Zul did not know that the animals had already arrived to answer the call of a dead or dying man. And as Troy made a decision of his own, he was answered by a thrust of emotion from the seemingly empty spaces of the room—fear, such as had moved the kinkajou to his arms in the garden, a determination to fight, perhaps, too, a vague plea. And he knew that he was again tuned in on the hidden five. If the animals had been used by Kyger in some scheme, certainly they had only been tools.

"Let the patrollers get them," Zul continued, "and they will have them under probes to learn what they can—and kill them afterwards. Is it not better to kill them cleanly before that is done?"

Troy stiffened, felt his own reaction intensified as

115

the others picked it up. What Zul said made such good sense it presented a new form of danger, and a very big one. But his own thoughts were racing ahead.

So far only those in this room knew that Kyger was dead, with the exception of his killer—which gave Troy a small measure of time. He knew that he could not let Zul kill the animals, and he would fight to keep them from falling into the hands of those who would wring secrets out of them via the probes.

Flight— But where? Memory painted for him a picture of that plateau high in the clean wind. Not perhaps there—but the Wild that stretched over half of this continent. To shake one man and five small animals out of that would be a long and arduous task and before it was done perhaps he could find a solution to their problem in another way.

"You'll have to let me call them—and kill them quickly!" Zul was losing control, his voice rasping louder as he watched Troy with narrowed eyes.

"Be quiet!" Troy enforced that order by planting his hand over the other's mouth. Holding Zul so in spite of his renewed writhings, Horan tried to contact the animals.

"Go together—away from here." He thought those words with all the emphasis he could, not trying to analyze why he must champion the five, only knowing that it was very important to do so—not only for them but for him.

If Zul understood what he was doing, he gave no sign of it. As he fought to be free of Troy's hold, his eyes were now wild above the temporary gag of the other's palm.

There was again a flicker of movement, which Troy

caught only from the corners of his eyes. The black cat materialized as if from the flooring, came stealthily, with its belly fur brushing the carpet, skirting Kyger's outflung arm. And Zul, sighting it over Troy's hand, was still. Troy waited as the cat reached them, to front Zul with a silent, menacing snarl, hatred expressed in every fluid line of its body.

"They do not need to be called, Zul," Troy said softly, "for they are here. And from here they shall go safely."

So they came—the other cat in a swift spring, the foxes side by side, and last of all the kinkajou in a rush that brought it to Troy, to climb up his body as if it were a tree.

"We shall all go together for a little, Zul." Troy swung the smaller man about, held him before him with one hand as he transferred Zul's knife to his own belt. He dropped the tube to the floor, and the black cat went into instant action, setting it rolling with small paw taps until the cylinder disappeared under one of the cabinets. Now all the animals, save the kinkajou which rode on Troy's shoulder, its tail loosely coiled about the man's neck, slipped out the door.

Zul might have been shocked speechless by the appearance of that furred company and their cooperation with Troy. He obeyed the other's push like a controlled robot, and all his struggles ceased as they went down the stairs, heading toward the courtyard.

One part of Troy's mind considered the matter of supplies—and the flitter. So much depended now on chance and luck, and he would have to hope for help from both.

Still holding Zul, he paused just within the passage

door and looked out into the courtyard. The flitter was just where he had seen it last. From the pens and cages came the usual night sounds. And there was no sign of the yardman who should have been on duty.

Troy caught a stir at the side of the flitter, knew that the animals had picked that much of his intention from his mind. At this hour the air lanes would be crowded with villa dwellers returning home from night spots in Tikil. He would have that traffic for cover from the patrollers.

Now that he had made his decision, Troy had to throttle down the excitement bubbling in him. For the first time in years he was going to sample freedom. He had had a very small taste of that on the expedition with Rerne, but this time the choice was his alone.

Zul remained the immediate problem. Troy continued to propel the other before him until they reached the storeroom. Since they had left the room in which Kyger lay, the other had not struggled. It might have been that he had no more desire than Troy to draw attention to their activities.

Inside, Troy shoved his captive into a corner and worked fast. He knew that Kyger had made a point of supplying the Terran animals with special imported food, and he tossed into a sack such containers of that as he could find. Zul's knife was in his belt and in addition the flitter would have a stunner in its arms locker. He drew the cord of the sack tight, with Zul watching him. The latter spoke and Troy knew he meant every word he said.

"We shall hunt and we shall kill. And the patrollers will hunt also. There is no place you can hide that one

118

or the other of us will not find. And for you also there will be death now."

"Because I know too much?" Troy suggested.

"Because of that—and because of this. We cannot allow knowledge of this thing."

"And you will set the patrollers on me—"

Zul grinned. "There will be no need to tell them of the animals. They will come and find a dead man where one of his hirelings has fled. That is a story that needs no telling, even to the most stupid."

"Suppose they find that two have fled?" Troy asked. He had no wish to take Zul along; that would be like fitting a triggered egg bomb into the flitter. But the disappearance of two of Kyger's employees at the same time, and one of them an old associate of the ex-spacer, might mud ly the trail as far as the law was concerned.

Slinging the bag over his shoulder, he closed on Zul again, herding him out of the storeroom in the direction of the flitter. But that plan was to go awry. There was a sudden shout from the passage leading to Kyger's quarters. Zul relaxed, made himself a dead weight that Troy could not hope to manhandle into the flyer without a loss of precious time. He leaped over the prone man and scrambled into the flitter, hoping the animals were already on board.

"Here!" Out of nowhere came that reassurance as Troy took the lift control and raised the machine out of the well of the courtyard. Lights showed in the forepart of Kyger's rooms. Perhaps one of the yardmen had discovered the body. Troy must make the best use of the small head start that he had.

The main stream of the late traffic went north, not east, and he would have to weave into that, not making the necessary turn until he was well over the villa section. Also the flitter must keep within the lawful speed of the passenger lanes.

Troy triggered the com on the control panel and listened intently for any hint that the alarm had been raised behind him. Zul's words had not been an idle threat. However, once in the Wild, he did not fear the patrollers too much.

What did concern him was the Clan rangers, organized to track down just such unauthorized invasions as his own. They knew the wilderness intimately. This realization made future prospects suddenly far more bleak for Troy, and they grew grimmer the farther he flew. Yet he had made his choice and there was no turning back.

Rerne! If cornered, dare he appeal to the Hunter? Once more he experienced the odd duality he had known that morning on the plateau. Part of him was untrusting, wary, disillusioned, and another segment pulled toward confidence in the ranger, a longing for the freedom in which he and his kind walked under an open sky.

A patroller cruised above his flitter, and Troy sat stiff and tense, waiting for the order to land. Then the official flyer darted away, and he drew a really deep breath once more. The traffic about him was thinning. Soon he would have to make his dash out of the regular lanes into what he hoped would be the concealment of the night. He saw the twinkle of villa lights, two of them among the rising heights. Snapping off his lawful lights, he banked to the right, coming

120

around to head eastward in a burst of speed that should tear him well away from the city lanes before he was noticed.

But it was several very long moments before he could be sure of that escape. So far there had been no warning broadcast on the com. Certainly if the men in the shop had been aroused, they would have called in the patrollers and there would be a blanket alarm out for the stolen flitter. Zul—was Zul still determined to hold off the law as long as he could to serve his own purposes?

And in the last warning the little man had said "we"—not "I". Who were "we"? If Kyger was not the master of the animals—and Zul was certainly a subordinate—then who was? Someone in Tikil with power enough to delay the official hunt so that a private and deadly one could be put into motion? Zul had warned Troy that he would be the quarry of two chases. And in the Wild perhaps tailed by the Clans as well.

Troy's lips shaped a mirthless smile. Too many hunting parties might just foul each other. He would not speculate on chances that might not exist. One move at a time was all anyone could make.

The flitter sped on into the night, northeast. Before daylight caught them and he would have to set down, they should be well into the wilderness. And, remembering the mountain chains Rerne had lifted them above, he set the flyer to climbing, though the automatic alarm system was on and the autopilot would avoid any crash against an unseen peak.

He became conscious of warmth against his thigh and side, the soft touch of a small paw on his nervously

121

rigid arm. The kinkajou was pressed against him, and the rest of that odd crew had climbed into the other half of the driver's seat. Troy began to talk, not knowing how much of what he said reached their minds, but driven by the impulse to put his nebulous plans into words.

"There is the Wild ahead—and only the rangers and the native animals in it. Such a place should hold many hiding places for such as we—"

"And good hunting." From one of them had come that quick reply. He sensed a rising excitement that was born not of fear or the need for defense but of anticipation—an emotion that all five of them shared.

"Good hunting." He confirmed that. "Trees, and plains, mountains, rivers, rocks—"

"It is good to run free." Out of the general aura of satisfaction those definite words arose.

"It is good to run free!" Troy echoed. Free of the Dipple, of Tikil—of the ways of men, which he had endured only because of his own stubborn determination not to be broken.

Overhead the stars made a clear, cold pattern, and the green round of the moon, rising above the mountains, showed snow caps like clear jade. The fugitives were across the first rim of the Larsh—into the Wild—and still no hint that the chase was up behind. Troy knew again the heady exultation of one who is pulling off an odds-against mission. He had no map, no points of reference, but he was certain that to simply continue northeast would bring him out along the fringe of the plains.

He set the controls on complete autopilot, stretched his arms wide. His shoulders ached from the rigid tension that had held him during the first hours of flight.

"By dawn," he told his companions, "we shall be down—in a big country where there are no trails."

The kinkajou had crowded into his lap, was curling up against him. And now the black cat was at his side, sitting upright, watching the night sky outside the bubble of the flitter, as if it had now accepted Troy as one of its own kind.

He must have drowsed, for the red snap of light on the control panel brought him awake with the stupid dullness of a too quickly aroused sleeper.

"Warn off! Warn off!"

Troy had heard just that same metallic voice before, but he could not remember when or why.

His hands went to the controls. He thumbed the autopilot release, but it did not give. As he hammered at it with his fist, that blink of light became steady and he remembered—Ruh—karv!

"Warn off!"

Troy reached for the mike, to say the words that would end their escape attempt. But that move came too late. The red light was now a beam. Out of the night blossomed a huge burst of eye-searing white. The flitter lurched, lost speed, started down.

Eleven

Afterwards Troy could recall little of that crazy falling-leaf descent that threw them from one side of the pilot's seat to the other. They were not quite helpless before the force that had shaken them off course and out of the sky, for the accident-safety ray had flashed on automatically, bringing them down to ground level at a speed under that of a direct crash. Troy fought the controls, beat at the lock with the full force of his wrists and arms. Something gave and for an instant or so the flitter was his again. He tried to put the nose up and the flyer gave a giant hop.

If that action did not win them the sky again, it did carry the flyer—with the effect of bursting through a taut curtain—beyond the influence of the thing that had grabbed them out of the air. Troy felt the flitter wheels strike, bouncing them up. They flattened off in a second crash, and it was dark—moon and stars blotted out.

His chest hurt and his head ached. In his mouth was the unforgettable flat sweet taste of blood. Before him was darkness, but from behind came a measure of light that he could sight as he tried to turn his head.

"Out—out—" That was a plea rising to a kind of frenzy. Troy could feel movement beside him, back and forth across his bruised body until he grunted with pain.

124

Somehow he forced up his left arm, worked at the catch of the cabin door, lunging against that stubborn barrier with the strength of his shoulder. The panel gave, tumbling him out, and small paws thudded on him as their owners raced into the open.

Troy pulled himself up and tried to see where they had come to earth. Under him the surface of the ground seemed singularly smooth. His hand, questing over it, scraped up the grit of sand that lay in a drifted skim on stone or rock, very level stone or rock. As he twisted fully around, he could see the shaft of moonlight better. Behind—yes—the flitter had in some incredible way fitted itself nose first into a crevice where an arch of roof shut off the sky.

Troy worked his way around the wreckage to the light. But it was after he had crawled those few feet that he realized what had happened and how chance, the protective device of the Clans, and his own last-moment attempt to control the flitter had landed them in an unusual hiding place. Those rounded domes and crumbling walls, blind of any window or door opening were set deep in the sand of a desert waste. He had crashed straight into the heart of Ruhkarv itself!

"Where—?" He tried to summon the animals—and since he had no names to call, he pictured them mentally. The cats, black and gray-blue, the foxes, russet and cream, the kinkajou, where were they? Hurt? Still about?

"Come—come back!" He called softly aloud, heard odd echoes reply from the ruins about. Outside now, he could look around, see how the flyer had nosed into a dome that had a crumbled opening in one side.

A shadow leaped from one of the broken arches,

125

pattered to him. The kinkajou had answered his call. It leaped to his shoulder, coiling its flexible tail about his upper arm in a grip tight enough to pinch. Troy reached up his other hand, caressed the round head butting against his cheek.

Then the foxes returned in a swift lope, stopping before him, their pointed noses up, testing the wind, their eyes agleam.

"Come," Troy coaxed the cats. When there was no answer, he detached the kinkajou, started back into the dome cave to explore the wreck. In the pocket of the door he had wrenched open he found an atom torch and thumbed its button. The cone of light made clear the nose of the flyer embedded in the space of the dome as a too thick thread might have been forced into the eye of a needle.

Troy flashed the light into the machine and then stood very still as he saw a small limp body. Blue eyes wide with pain were raised to his. The gray-blue cat lay flat, its mouth open, panting. Now and again it licked a foreleg that was clamped tight between two buckled pieces of metal. Above it crouched its black mate, who, upon seeing Troy, uttered a series of sharp, demanding cries.

Setting down the torch, Troy went to work to free the delicate leg. Then he carried the cat into the open, placing it on the ground until he could salvage the aid kit of the flyer.

By the time the first thin streaks of false dawn were in the sky, he had done what he could. The leg had been set and treated. He had dragged out of the flitter the food bag, the stunner, and some of the kit tools, which he festooned from his own belt. As time had passed and no one had invaded the forbidden area of the ruins to gather them up prisoners, Troy began to believe that they had been brought down by some automatic guard device and that on foot they still had a chance to escape capture. But whether the Clans had set other guards about Ruhkarv, which might now keep them inside, he did not know.

The foxes and the black cat melted into the shadows, leaving Troy to his collection of equipment. Only the kinkajou remained to watch and at last to come to his aid, dragging small objects from the wrecked flyer to pile by the dome. Troy sat back on his heels. He had been so busy that he had not had time to consider the future further than the next job to be done, for he had been driven by a sense of working against time.

"Wall—wall that cannot be seen—" The black cat stepped out from a neighboring dome and came directly to the man.

"Wall around here?" Troy's hand swept in a gesture to indicate the ruins.

"Yes. We have tried to cross many places."

One of Troy's fears had materialized. The Clans must have set a barrier about Ruhkarv. Intended to bar interlopers, it would make him and the animals prisoners within. How he had managed to pierce it with the flitter was a mystery.

"There are many dens—maybe hunting in them—" One of the foxes drifted into the open. The cat had gone to its injured mate, was licking its head caressingly.

"Danger underground here." Troy countered that half suggestion from the prick-eared scout.

"Not now." The report was emphatic and Troy wondered. Before Fauklow's expedition with the recaller

127

had turned the name of Ruhkarv into a synonym for nightmare, the upper galleries of the strange city or structure had been explored with impunity by a handful of the curious. If it had been only the action of the recaller that had damned the place—well, the rangers had put an end to the machine's broadcasts, according to Rerne, and the undersurface passages might give the fugitives shelter for a time. He would have to have some rest, Troy knew, and perhaps here in the heart of a forbidden territory they had found temporary safety after all.

"We go then—to a safe den."

With the food bag over his shoulder, the injured cat held as comfortably as he could manage against his chest, and the stunner ready in his free hand, Troy moved out. The kinkajou rode on his shoulder, making small twittering noises and now and then patting its two-legged steed with a forepaw as if to make Troy continually aware of its presence. The foxes and the black cat guided him to another dome, in which a large segment of wall had been cut through in the past, either by one of the early treasure seekers or by the ill-fated Fauklow men.

All the fantastic tales that had been told of this place were peopling the dusk Troy faced with a myriad of nightmares, but the readiness of the animals to explore was his insurance. Troy knew that their senses were far keener and more to be relied upon than his own, and that they would give warning of any trouble ahead. He snapped on the atom torch he had slung from his belt, watched the cone of light bob and wave across flooring and walls as it swung to the rhythm of his walk.

128

There was nothing to be seen but walls and a pavement of blocks, fitted together with precision and skill. At the far side of the dome was the dark mouth of a ramp leading down into the real Ruhkarv. That murk had a quality close to fog, Troy thought—as if the dark itself swirled about with independent motion. And even the atom light was sapped, weakened by it. Yet the lead fox had already padded down into those depths, and its mate and the cat were waiting for Troy almost impatiently.

"This is a place where there has been great danger," Troy warned, combining words with the mental reach.

"Nothing here—" He was sure that impatient overtone came from the black cat.

"Nothing here," Troy repeated even as his boots clicked on that sloping length of stone, "but perhaps farther on—"

"There is water."

Troy was startled at that confident interruption. They had the supplies from the flitter, but the problem of water had nagged at him. If somewhere within this maze the animals had located water, they were even better provided for than he had dared to hope.

"Where?"

"We go—"

The ramp carried him down through three levels of side corridors, all empty as far as the beams of the atom light could disclose, all exactly alike, so that Troy began to think a man might well become lost in such a place without a guide. And he tried to set his own entrance path in his head, memorizing each corridor by counting.

Somewhere there must be an unseen air system, for

129

the atmosphere, though dry and acrid, remained breathable, and he was sure that now and then from one of the offshoot corridors he scented a whiff of some fresh import from the surface.

At the fourth level, though the ramp continued on to Korwarian depths, Troy found the three scouts waiting for him. And now, unless his sense of direction was completely bemused, they took a way that headed directly east. For a moment he dared to wonder if some one of these long hallways might not take them outside the range of the blocking-wave wall so that they could emerge free in the Wild.

Stark walls of red-gray stone, paved footing—nothing else, save the fine sifting of centuries of dust, which arose almost ankle-high and muffled the sounds of his own footfalls. Twice only were those walls broken by round openings, but when he swung the beam of the torch in, he saw nothing save a bare, circular cell hardly large enough for a man to crouch in, without any other opening. The purpose of such rooms—if rooms they could be called—remained another of the Ruhkarv mysteries.

But their journey was not to continue so easily. The eastern corridor ended in a huge well, and again a descending ramp faced them, curving about the side of that opening, narrow enough to make Troy thoughtful, though the slope was not too steep as far as he could sight with the torch's aid. Again the scouts moved ahead, and there was nothing to do except follow.

As he went down, there was a change in the air—not a freshness, but a rise of moisture. As the wall against which he steadied himself from time to time began to grow clammy under his fingers, he knew that the fox
130

had been right. Somewhere below was a source of water—a large one, if he could judge by the present evidence.

As the moisture content grew, he was aware of a fetid under scent—not exactly the stagnant stench of an undrained and unrenewed pond under the sun, but the hint of something ill about that water. However, there were trickles of damp on the walls and his thirst grew.

Around and around—the coiled spring of the ramp inside the well began to form a dizzying pattern. There was no break here made by side corridors. Troy lost track of time; his legs ached, and every bruise on his body added to his punishment. He was sure now that if he should try to reverse his path and reach the surface—or even the last corridor from which this drop had issued, he would not be able to summon up strength enough to finish. There was only the need to get to the bottom of the well, out on the level somewhere where he could drop down and rest.

And finally the torch did show him a pavement. Troy reached it in a long stride and flashed the light about the bottom of the well. There was water right enough, but—as dry as his mouth now was, as much as his body cried out for a drink—he could not bring himself to approach closely that sullenly flowing runnel.

The water was a ribbon of oily black, looking as thick and turgid as if the substance were more than half slime, and it moved with sluggish ripples on its surface from one side of the pit to the other, filling to within a few inches of the pavement surface a stone trough that had been constructed to carry it.

The inlet and outlet for that yard-wide flow were

large circular openings—the inlet situated under the rise of the ramp from the floor. And except for those there was no other way out—save the ramp down which he had just come. But the black cat and the foxes were at the mouth of the inflow tunnel, and when Troy walked to that point, he saw that the tunnel was larger than the stream at floor level, leaving a narrow path to the right of the water.

"Out?" he asked, and that single word echoed hollowly until the boom hurt his ears. The kinkajou chattered angrily, and the cat in Troy's hold pressed the good foreleg hard against his chest and added a protesting wail. But the three animals before him glanced up and then away again, into the tunnel, telling him as plainly as with words or the mind touch that this was indeed the proper exit.

The ripples on the water, as Troy passed along so close to it, began to take on a rather ominous and sinister significance, and he wondered just how deep that trough really was, for some of the ripples went against the current, suggesting action under the dark surface of the flood—something or things moving independently against the flow of the water. For an anxious while one such V of ripples accompanied Troy at his own pace. Time and time again he paused to flash the torch directly on that disturbance—to sight nothing in the inky liquid.

That slight fetid odor was growing stronger, yet again he felt a puff of renewing air, though through what channel in the walls he could not guess. But the gleam of his torch began to pick up small answering sparks of light along the walls. From pinpricks scattered without apparent pattern they grew thicker, set in clusters. And once, when he turned his head to watch a particularly large and suspicious line of ripples, Troy saw that those sparks of light behind him, awakened by the torchlight, did not lose their gleam but continued as small patches with a bluish glow. He tried the experiment of snapping the torch off for a moment and looked about him. Where the atom light had touched, that blue glow remained. But ahead the way was still dark. Whatever those flecks might be, they needed the radiance from the light to set them actually working.

The patches of such light grew larger, and now he thought he could trace a kind of design—like a sharply peaked zigzag—in their general setting, which argued that they were not native to the rock blocks of which these walls were fashioned but placed there with a purpose by the unknown builders. At last he was backed by an eerie glow walling in the stream along which he walked.

His torch found an opening in the wall ahead. The cat awaited him there, but the foxes were not to be seen. Troy pushed on, eager to be out of the tunnel and its attendant water channel.

When he came out, he was not in another corridor or room—but he stepped into what might have once been some vast underground cavern adapted by the unknown builders of Ruhkarv to their own peculiar uses. His torch beam was swallowed up by the vastness of the open expanse and he halted, a little daunted by what faced him. Here was a city in miniature, open ways running between walls of separate, roofless enclosures. And yet the substance of those walls—! It was from here that the fetid odor had come. He could

133

not be sure, yet somehow he shrank from putting his guess to the test of actually laying his hand upon one of those slimily moist surfaces—but it looked at first, and even after a more careful examination, as if those walls grew out of the ground, that they were giant slabs of an unknown fungus.

There was an open space of white-gray soil, neither sand nor gravel but possessing a granular appearance, between the mouth of the water tunnel and the beginning of the first of those structures, and Troy was in no hurry to cross it.

"A road around—"

One or all of his guides had picked his feelings of repugnance out of his mind, and he knew then that they shared it in a measure.

"Come!" The last was urgent and Troy broke into a clumsy trot, not sure now just how long he could keep moving at all. He rounded an outthrust suburb of the fungus town and saw something else—a shaft of brightness that was so clean, so much of the world that he knew, that he threw himself toward it, his trot lengthening into a run.

There was an island of sanity in the midst of what was not of his world, nor, he suspected, of any human world. From some break in the arch overhead, through what unknown trick of nature—or of the architects of this place—he would never know, a shaft of sun struck here. And there was water, a small pool of it fed by a runnel through the sand. Clear water with none of the turgid rolling of the stream that had led them here. Troy put down the injured cat where it could lap beside its mate, scooped up a palmful to wet lips and chin as he sucked avidly.

Two, three tiny plants, frail as lace, grew on the bank of that pool. Troy drank again blissfully and then opened the supply bag, sharing its contents among his band, taking himself the concentrates that would give him days of energy.

Was there any other way out of this dead, fungoid world? At the moment he was too tired to care. With his head pillowed on the food bag, Troy curled up, weak with exhaustion, aware that the animals were gathering in about him, as if they, too, distrusted what lay beyond the circle of sunlight.

Did anything live here? The ripples in the water had been suggestive. And there might be other creatures to whom the fungus-walled streets were home. But Troy could no longer summon the strength to stand guard. He felt the warmth of small furred bodies pressed against his, and that was the last he remembered.

Twelve

He might have been asleep only for a moment, Troy thought when he roused. The sun patch still lit the pool. There had been no change in his surroundings, save that the animals, except for the injured cat, were gone. The cat raised its head from licking the splinted leg and made an inquiring noise deep in its throat as Horan sat up, rubbing his arm across his eyes. He shook his head, still a little bemused, wondering vaguely if he had slept the clock around.

Then out of the murk of the fungus growth trotted the black cat, its head held high as it dragged the body of a limp thing across the coarse earth. Paying no attention to Troy, it brought the weird underground dweller to its mate.

The dead creature was in its way as hideous as the hur-hur, a nightmare combination of many legs, stalked eyes, segmented, plated body. But apparently to both felines it was a very acceptable form of food and they dined amiably together.

If the Terran animals were able to forage for themselves even in this hole in the ground, Troy had proof of another of Kyger's secrets. They had *not* needed the special food that had been so ceremoniously delivered at a suitably high price to the quondam owners in Tikil.

"Good hunting?" he asked the black casually.

The cat was engaged in a meticulous toilet with tongue and paw.

"Good hunting," it agreed.

"The others also have good hunting?" Troy wondered where in that unwholesome fungoid growth the missing three hunted and what they pursued.

"They eat," the cat answered with finality.

Troy stood up, stretched the cramps out of his sore body. He had no intention of remaining in this cavern, or underground city, or whatever it might be.

"There is a way out?" he asked the cat, and received the odd mental equivalent of what might have been a shrug. It was plain that hunting had been of more importance than exploration for another passage as far as that independent animal was concerned.

Troy sat down again to study both cats. The injured one was still eating, with neatness, but hungrily. He was sure that it was not unaware of the exchange between its mate and himself.

Horan had no control over the five Terran animals, and he knew it. By some freak of chance he was able to communicate with them after a disjointed fashion. But he was very sure that their communication with Kyger had been much clearer and fuller—perhaps through the aid of that odd summoning device he had seen in the dead man's hands.

They had accompanied him in the flight from Tikil because that had suited their purpose also, just as they had guided him to this particular hole. Yet he knew well that if they wished they would leave him as readily, unless he could establish some closer tie with them. The position was changed—in Tikil he had been in command because that was man's place. Here the animals had found their own; they no longer needed him.

It was disquieting to face the fact that his somewhat rosy dreams of cooperation between man and animal might be just that—dreams. He could fly the fussel to his will and that bird would know the pleasure of the hunt and still return on call. But these hunters had wills and minds of their own, and if they gave companionship, it would be by free will. The age-old balance of man and animal had tipped. There would be a cool examination from the other side, no surrender but perhaps an alliance.

And such thoughts could lead Troy now to understand

Zul's demand that the animals be killed. Few men were going to accept readily a copartnership with creatures they had always considered property. There would lurk a threat to the supremacy man believed in.

Yet Troy knew that he could not have left any of the animals in Tikil, nor yielded to Zul's demands. Why? Why did he feel that way about them? He was uneasy now, almost unhappy, as he realized that he was not dealing with pets, that he must put aside his conception of these five as playthings to be owned and ordered about. Neither were they humans whose thinking processes and reactions he could in a manner anticipate.

The black cat ceased its toilet, sat upright, the tip of its tail folded neatly over its paws, its blue eyes regarding Troy. And the man stirred uneasily under that unwinking stare.

"You wish a way out?"

"Yes." Troy answered that simply. With this new humbleness he was willing to accept what the other would give.

"This place—not man's—not ours—"

Troy nodded. "Before man—something like man but different."

"There is danger—old danger here." There was a new touch of thought like a new voice. The gray-blue cat had finished its meal and was looking over the good paw, raised to its mouth for a tonguing, at Troy.

"There was a bad thing happened here to men—some years ago."

Both cats appeared to consider that. Perhaps their minds linked in a thread of communication he could not reach.

138

"You are not of those we know." That was the black cat. Troy discovered that he could now distinguish one's thought touch from another's. The animals had come to be definite and separate personalities to him and closer in companionship because of that very fact. Sometimes he was so certain of a comrade at hand that it was a shock to realize that the mind he could touch was outwardly clothed in fur and was borne by four feet, not two.

"No."

"Few men know our speech—and those must use the caller. Yet from the first you could contact us without that. You are a different kind of man." That was the gray-blue cat.

"I do not know. You mean that you cannot 'talk' to everyone?"

"True. To the big man we talked—because that was set upon us—just as we had to obey the caller when he used it. But it was not set upon us to talk to you—yet you heard. And you are not one-who-is-to-be-obeyed."

Set upon them—did they mean that they had been conditioned to obey orders and "talk" with certain humans?

"No," Troy agreed. "I do not know why I hear your 'talk,' but I do."

"Now that the big man is gone, we are hunted."

"That is so."

"It is as was told us. We should be hunted if we tried to be free."

"We are free," the black cat interrupted. "We might leave you, man, and you could not find us here unless we willed it so."

"That is true."

Again the pause, those unblinking stares. The black cat moved. It came to him, its tail erect. Then it sat upon its hind legs. Horan put out his hand diffidently, felt the quick rasp of a rough tongue for an instant on his thumb.

"There will be a way out."

The cat's head turned toward the fungus town. It stared as intently in that direction as it had toward Troy a moment earlier. And the man was not surprised when out of that unwholesome maze trotted the fox pair, followed by the kinkajou. They came to stand before Troy, the black cat a little to one side, and the man caught little flickers of their unheard speech.

"Not one-to-be-obeyed—hunts in our paths—will let us walk free—"

It was the black cat who continued as spokesman. "We shall hunt your way for you now, man. But we are free to go."

"You are free to go. I share my path; I do not order you to walk upon it also." He searched for phrases to express his acceptance of the bargain they offered and his willingness to be bound by their conditions.

"A way out—" The cat turned to the others. The foxes lapped at the pool and then loped away. The kinkajou dabbled its front paws in the water. Troy offered it a pressed-food biscuit and it ate with noisy crunchings. Then it turned to the cavern wall at their back and frisked away along its foot.

"We shall go this way." The cat nodded to the right of the pool, along that clean strip of ground between the fungoid growth and the cavern wall.

Troy emptied two of the containers of dry food, rinsed them, and filled them with water as a reserve supply.

140

Both cats drank slowly. Then Troy picked up the injured one, who settled comfortably in the crook of his arm. The black darted away.

Horan walked at a reasonable pace, studying his surroundings as he went. To the glance there was no alteration in either the fungus walls or the rock barrier to his right. But as he drew farther away from the splotch of sunlight, he switched on his atom torch.

The cat stirred in his hold, its head—with ears sharply pointed—swung to face the fungus.

"There is something there—alive?" Troy's hand went to the stunner in a belt loop.

"Old thing—not alive," the thought answer came readily. "Sargon finds—"

"Sargon?"

The wavering picture of the male fox crossed his mind. "You are named?" he asked eagerly. Somehow names made them seem less aloof and untouchable, closer to his own kind.

"Man's names!" There was disdain in that, hinting that there were other forms of identification more subtle and intelligent, beyond the reach of a mere human. And Troy, reading that into the cat's reply, smiled.

"But I am a man. May I not use man's names?"

The logic of that appealed to the dainty lady he carried. "Sargon and Sheba." Fleeing fox faces flashed into his mind. "Shang"—that was the kinkajou. "Simba, Sahiba," her mate and herself.

"Troy Horan," he answered gravely aloud, to complete the round of introduction. Then he came back to her report. "This old thing—it was made—or did it once live?"

141

"It once lived." Sahiba relayed the fox's report promptly. "It was not man—not we—different."

Troy's curiosity was aroused, not enough, however, to draw him into the paths threading the forbidding fungoid town. But as they passed that point he wondered if the remains of one of the original inhabitants of Ruhkarv could lie there.

"An opening—" Sahiba relayed a new message. "Shang has discovered an opening—up—" She pointed with her good paw to the cavern wall.

Troy altered course, came up a slight slope, and found the kinkajou chattering excitedly and clinging head down to a knob that overhung a crevice in the wall. Troy flashed the torch into that dark pocket. There was no rear barrier; it was a narrow passage. Yet it did not have any facing of worked stone as had the other corridor entrances, and it might not lead far.

The foxes and Simba came from different directions and stood sniffing the air in the rocky slit. Troy was conscious of that too—a faint, fresh current, stirring the fetid breath of the fungus, hinting of another and cleaner place. This must be a way out.

Yet the waiting animals did not seem in any hurry to take that path.

"Danger?" asked Troy, willing to accept their hesitation as a warning.

Simba advanced to the overhang of the opening, his head held high, his whiskers quivering a little, as he investigated by scent.

"Something waiting—for a long time waiting—"

"Man? Animal?"

But Simba appeared baffled. "A long time waiting," he repeated. "Maybe no longer alive—but still waiting."

Troy tried to sift some coherent meaning out of that. The kinkajou made him start as it leaped from the rock perch to his shoulder.

"It is quiet." Shang broke in over Simba's caution. "We go outside—this way outside—"

But Troy asked Simba for the final verdict. "Do we go?"

The cat glanced up at him, and there was a flash of something warm upon the meeting of their eyes, as if Troy in his deference to the other's judgment had advanced another step on the narrow road of understanding between them.

"We go—taking care. This thing I do not understand."

The foxes were apparently content to follow Simba's lead. And the three trotted into the crevice, while Troy came behind, the atom torch showing that this way was indeed a slit in the rock wall and no worked passage.

Though the break was higher than his head by several feet, it was none too wide, and Troy hoped that it would not narrow past his using. Now that he was well inside and away from the cavern, the freshness of the air current blowing softly against his face was all the more noticeable. He was sure that in that breeze was the scent of natural growing things and not just the mustiness of the Ruhkarv paths.

They had not gone far before the pathway began to slope upward, confirming his belief that it connected somehow with the outside world. At first, that slope was easy, and then it became steeper, until at last Troy was forced to transfer Sahiba to the ration bag on his back and use both hands to climb some sections. His less sensitive nose registered more than just fresh

143

air now. There was an unusual fragrance, which was certainly not normal in this slit of rock, more appropriate to a garden under a sun hot enough to draw perfume from aromatic plants and flowers. Yet beneath that almost cloying scent lay a hint of another odor, a far less pleasant one—the flowers of his imagining might be rooted in a slime of decay.

The torch showed him another climb. Luckily the surface was rough and furnished handholds. Shang and Simba went up it fluidly, the foxes in a more scrambling fashion. Then Troy reached the top and was greeted by a glow of daylight. He snapped off the torch and advanced eagerly.

"No!" That warning came emphatically from more than one of the animals. Troy stiffened, studied the path ahead, saw now that between him and the open was a grating or mesh of netting.

He stood still. The cat and the foxes were outlined clearly against that mesh.

"Gone—"

A flicker of thought, which was permission for him to come on. There *was* a meshwork over the way into the open. And through it he could see vegetation and a brightness that could only be daylight. The mesh itself was of a sickly white color and was formed in concentric rings with a thick blob like a knob in the center.

Troy approached it gingerly, noting that the cat and the foxes did not get within touching distance. Now he noticed something else—that along the rings of the netting were the remains of numerous insects, ragged tatters of wings, scraps of carcasses, all clinging to the

144

surface of those thick cords. He drew the knife from his belt and sliced down with a quick slash, only to have the cord give very slightly beneath his blow. Then the blade rebounded as if he had struck at some indestructible elastic substance.

The cord stuck to the blade so that it was carried upward on the rebound, and he had to give a hard jerk to free it. A second such experiment nearly pulled the knife out of his grasp. Not only was the stuff elastic and incredibly tough, but it was coated with something like glue, and he did not think it was any product of man—or of man's remote star-born cousins.

There was clearly no cutting through it. But there was another weapon he could use. Troy set down the bag in which Sahiba rode and investigated the loot he had brought with him from the wrecked flitter. There was a small tube, meant originally for a distress flare, but with another possible use.

Troy examined the webbing as well as he could without touching it. The strands were coated with thick beads of dust. It had been in place there for a long time. Unscrewing the head of the flare and holding the other end of the tube, he aimed it at the center of the web.

Violent red flame thrust like a spear at the net. There was an answering flower of fire running from the point of impact along the cords to their fastening points on the rock about the opening, a stench that set Troy to coughing. Then—there was nothing at all fronting them but the open path and some trails of smoke wreathing from the stone.

They waited for those to clear before Simba took

a running leap to cross the fire-blackened space, the foxed following him eagerly. Troy, again carrying Sahiba and Shang, brought up the rear.

He was well away from the cliff before he realized that they might have made their escape from the cavern of the fungus town, but they were not yet on the open surface of Korwar. There was vegetation here, growing rankly in an approximation of sunlight, a light that filtered down from a vast expanse of roof crossed and crisscrossed with bars or beams set in zigzag patterns like those formed by the light sparks in the water tunnel. Between that patching of bars was a cream-white surface, which, seen from ground level, could have been sand held up by some invisible means.

As Troy studied that, he saw a puff of golden vapor exhaled from a section of crosshatched bars. The tiny cloud floated softly down until it was midway between the roof and earth, and then it discharged its bulk in a small shower, spattering big drops of liquid on the leaves of the plants immediately below.

And now Troy could see radical differences between those plants and the ordinary vegetation of the surface. Not far away a huge four-petaled flower—the petals a vivid cream, its heart a striking orange-red—hung without any stem Troy could detect, in a rounded opening among shaggy bushes.

The heavy, almost oppressive fragrance he had first noted in the passage came from that. Simba, nose extended, stalked toward the blossom. Then the cat arched its back and spat, its ears flattened to its skull. Troy, coming in answer to the wave of disgust and warning from the animal, found his boots crunching

146

the husks of small bodies, charnel house debris. His sickened reaction made him slice at the horrible flower—to discover it was not a flower but a cunning weave of sticky threads. And, as his knife blade tore through them, the orange-red heart came to life, leaping from the trap, darting straight at him.

Troy had a confused impression of many-legged thing with a gaping mouth, a thorned tail ready to sting. But Simba struck with a heavy clawed paw, throwing the creature up into the air. As it smashed to the ground, Sargon pounded it into the earth in a flattened smear. The fox sniffed and then drew back, his head down, his paws rubbing frantically at his nose.

Simba, tail moving in angry sweeps from side to side, sat half crouched as if awaiting a second attack.

"This is a bad place," Sahiba stated flatly. And Troy was ready to agree with her.

Oddly enough it was Shang, the kinkajou, who took the lead. He leaped from Troy's shoulder to the top of the nearest tall bush, and in a moment was only to be marked by a thrasing of branches as he headed into the miniature wilds. Troy dodged another made-to-order rain cloud and sat down to share out supplies with his oddly assorted company. They would need food and water before they tried to solve this latest riddle.

Thirteen

The same wild waving of leafed branches that had marked Shang's departure heralded his return. He made a flying leap from a nearby bush top to the ground, raising small spurts of dust as he raced toward Troy.

"Man thing!" There was excitement in that report, enough to make Troy set down a water container hastily, not quite sure whether Shang meant an animate or inanimate find.

"Where?" Troy asked, and then added quickly, "What?"

Shang raised a front paw and gestured to the miniature wilderness. He seemed unable to define the "what" at all. Troy looked to the cats; he had come to accept their superior judgment in such matters.

Simba faced the screen of vegetation, and Horan, alert now to the slight changes he might not have noted hours earlier, marked that twitch of whiskered muzzle. Sahiba, limping clumsily, left his side, joined her mate, and sat in the same listening attitude.

"Call thing—" It was Simba who reported.

Troy experienced a flicker of uneasiness. There had been a "call thing" associated with Ruhkarv, and he did not want to have any close connection with that, certainly not with what rumor and legend suggested that it had called.

148

"Old?" He did not know how Simba could pick the answer to that out of the air, or out of Shang and the messages the air brought feline senses.

"Not old."

"A man with it?"

Simba's blue eyes, with their unreadable depths, lifted from the foliage wall to Troy's. He caught the cat's puzzlement, as if Simba was able to pluck a confused series of impressions from channels closed to the man, but as if important sequences in that series were lacking.

"Man thing—" Shang was fairly dancing up and down with eagerness, running a few steps toward the wilderness, retreating to peer at Troy, plainly urging that his find be examined by Horan. But the man continued to wait for the cats' verdict.

"Dangerous?"

To that again neither Sahiba nor Simba made a direct answer. But the urge to caution was intensified. Then Sargon and Sheba went purposefully off into the brush as if obeying some order. Troy repacked the supplies, picked up Sahiba. He studied the matted growth before him, looking for a path, or at least a thinner patch through which he might force his way.

The light from the odd roofing overhead, which had been day-bright when he had found his way into this place, was fading, and Troy did not much relish plunging into the tangle. But, sighting a space between two bushes, he pushed in resolutely.

Within seconds he was completely lost. It was impossible to keep any sort of straight course, and he had to use his knife to get free of vines and sprawling branches. The whole growth might have been intelligently planted to form a giant trap or barrier. It was Sahiba who relayed the suggestions of the scouts and Shang who roamed from bush to bush, coming back to coax him on.

Then Troy half fell through a mass of foliage, as a tough vine gave way, and was once more in the open—facing a nightmare scene.

There was an opening in the wall here, with a well-cleared, paved space before it. And in the center of that, facing the opening, was a small machine, a machine akin to his own time and culture. A cone of meta-plast was pointed with its large end toward the wall opening, and, as Troy stepped onto the pavement, he was immediately conscious of the fact that a faint vibration came from that machine. It was not only in working order—it was running!

Cat, foxes, kinkajou—the animals were lined up well to the left of the machine, facing the opening—waiting—

Troy's cry was half choked in his throat as he looked beyond the machine, along the line of that pointed cone. It must—surely it must have once been human, that thing trembling a little, spread-eagled on just such a webbing as had choked the passage from the fungus cavern. Yet this was a dried rag-fashioned creature from which not only life but much of the bulk of body had vanished. The head, which still showed a thatch of dust-stiffened hair, lolled forward on the rack of bones that was the chest, and Troy was glad he could not see the features.

He surveyed the webbing, seeing not only that it covered the opening and held its long-dead prisoner upright, frail as that structure of skin and bones was, but that the cords also ran along the walls to form a pattern of stripes, some as fine as thread, others as thick as one of his fingers. And the thing that had woven the web could not have been one of the orange-red lily hearts. It must have been larger than the Terran animals.

Had been—must have been? What was there to prove that the weaver was now gone? The captive was dead. Troy thought he could guess how long he had been there—just as he knew what machine stood before them, its powers dampened out, mercifully, but still in operation. This was part of the horror that had put Ruhkarv out of bounds for his kind. The recaller had been set here, a point Fauklow had selected because his knowledge of nonhuman remains had indicated there might be a response. And there had been a response—too concrete a one.

Elsewhere the recaller had summoned only the pallid tatters of ghostly memories. Here some freak of time, space, or unknown nature had given body to a ghost and the power to use it! Out of a far and devious past and the corridors of Ruhkarv had come a creature, intelligent or not, ruler of those ways once, or a prowler in them, as great an enemy to the builders as it was to the Fauklow men, which had had the energy to revive and attack its arousers.

And perhaps the maker of that web had been only one of a number of monsters that had crawled out of the caverns of Ruhkarv. Most of the bodies of the explorers had been found aboveground with indications that they had, toward the end of their suffering, battled insanely against each other. Horrors driving them in a mad flight to the surface.

To the surface! That registered in Troy's mind now as he strove desperately to keep his imagination under control, to observe without trying to reconstruct what had happened here. Fauklow's men had set up the recaller, and they had fled from this point. So there was an exit to the surface somewhere from this chamber—did it lead through that opening before him?

He thought not. There would be no reason to aim the recaller on the back trail of the passage that had brought explorers here. No, that opening had had some significance for the dead archaeologist, but not as a door of escape. The old story of the treasure of Ruhkarv—had Fauklow found some clue that had led him to believe he could summon a whisper from the past to reveal the hiding place of the treasure?

Troy only knew that nothing would have led him to explore that dark tunnel mouth behind the spread and wasted body of a man who might have tried just that. He glanced at the animals. They were intent upon the scene, but not hostile.

"Dead only?" he asked.

Sahiba pushed back against his shoulder, her good foreleg rigid on his arm.

"Dead here—" But there remained an odd note of puzzlement in that reply.

"Here?" he echoed.

"It is here—yet it is not here." She shook her head.

Troy could not be sure of what she was trying to tell him. "The man is dead."

"Yes."

"And that which made the net?"

"It is"—the gray-blue head moved, soft fur rubbing his shoulder—"dead here—but waiting."

"The recaller!" Troy thought he knew now. Blanketed by the quencher beam from the rangers' installation, the machine could no longer materialize the uncanny thing from the past. But under that blanket the recaller still ran. Let anything again lift the quencher and the weaver of those webs would return!

Troy stared at the array of dials and buttons on the small control board set into the back of the machine. There was no way of his knowing which of those would close down the dangerous ray, and he had no intention of experimenting.

Simba crept slowly toward the web and the captive there. He might have been a hunter stalking prey. One black foreleg stretched, a paw with claws extended patted the drift of dust that lay at the foot of the webbing. Something bright spun from that dust and Simba followed it, keeping it rolling away from the opening, back, until it struck against Troy's boot.

The man stooped to pick it up. By the slick, cold feel he knew he held a ring of metal, a deep crimson-red. But as his fingers closed on it, there was a change in that plain blood-colored band. Sparks flashed on it, single and in pinpointed clusters, just as they had appeared on the walls of the water tunnel. And Troy believed that on his palm now rested no memento from the body of the unknown dead captive, but something that was native to these chambers and halls from the beginning, perhaps the only piece of the lost treasure of Ruhkarv that men of his own time would ever see. Had that, too, been summoned out of the past, given substance by some chance of the recaller? Or had it been found in the tunnel by the web captive, who had fled carrying it—only to be taken just as he was within sight of freedom?

On the band the sparks winked faster. Also—Troy frowned, completely puzzled. He had picked up a ring only a size too large for any of his fingers; now he was holding a much larger loop. Sahiba sniffed, then put out a paw, touched the hoop. It spanned his palm. Troy pushed his fingers together, inserted them. The band moved down, closed about his wrist, tightened there.

Startled, he jerked and tugged at it, only to find the bracelet now immovable, not tight enough to pinch the flesh, but resting as if it had been fashioned exactly to the measure of his arm. Yet under his exploring fingers the metal was solid surface, with no discernible joints or stretching bands to account for the alteration in size.

Sahiba patted it, apparently attracted by the winks of light still flickering on and off around it. Was it only a piece of personal ornamentation—or some outlandish weapon defensive or offensive?

"Good or bad?" he asked aloud, wondering if the acute senses of the animals could give him a reply to that.

"Old thing." Sahiba yawned.

"A way out?" Troy returned to the main problem. Perhaps some kind of trail would be marked in the earth of the garden away from this point. He walked along the edge of the pavement on which the recaller had been set, searching for any trace of the route taken coming or going by those who had brought the machine here and then must have fled or been driven back to the surface.

Simba and the foxes accompanied him, then darted

ahead, while Shang swung into the bushes again. They reached the end of that rectangle of pavement, and there Troy had eyes keen enough to pick out old scars of lopped branches, once again woven with a cloak of thick growth but still to be seen. He swung his knife, cutting a new way by those guides.

The light from overhead had dimmed into what was more night than dusk when he came out facing the foot of one of those ramps such as had led them down into this strange territory hours—or was it days?—earlier. He had lost all sense of time.

They made camp in a pocket of bare earth with the slope of the ramp at their backs. Troy eyed the now dark jungle distrustfully. So far only the lily hearts had been sighted as living things. But that did not mean that there were no other, just-as-vicious unknowns. And perhaps, as on the upper surface of Korwar, nocturnal hunters were more to be feared than those who stalked by day. Now more than ever he was dependent upon the senses of his companions. And that balance had shifted again—here man might be a liability to the Terrans.

He shared out supplies, noting that the animals made no move to hunt their own food.

"Hunting bad?"

Simba regarded the now gray-black mass of vegetation.

"There is hunting—for others—"

"Others—" That word might not echo in the air, but it did repeat itself in Troy's mind. He tried not to think of the captive in the web. Yes, there had been cruel hunting for others here.

"That which caught the man?" Against his will al-

155

most, Troy pressed the point. Did darkness activate what the recaller had summoned out of the past? With that thrust of apprehension, to be fed by his species' age-old distrust of the dark, Troy put out a hand to gather up the supply bag. Tired as he was, he had the atom torch, and he could keep going on the ramp until he dropped rather than face that weaver of webs. The residue of terror here bit at him now.

"No." Simba seemed assured of that. "Other things— this their place—"

As though on cue there came a cry out of the miniature jungle, a long, wavering screech that was made up of pain, terror, and the approach of death. Yet it was no cry that could have come from any animal he had ever known. And those he did know retreated, edging in around him, their heads turned to the jungle, their eyes alert, their lips lifted in snarls of warning.

"Out of here!" Troy's torch snapped on. "Up—"

He did not have to urge. The foxes sprang from the camp site to the ramp; the kinkajou was already racing after them. As Troy, carrying Sahiba and the bag, started that same climb, Simba fell in behind, looking back over his shoulder now and again, a low growl coming from his throat to warn off would-be trailers.

They went on climbing, the torch showing only the rise before them. Soon they were above the surface of the garden cavern, now in a sloping tunnel enclosed by rock walls.

They came to a level with corridors starring out at five different points, bare corridors in which his torch showed the dust disturbed, perhaps by the feet of the men who had planted the recaller and died for it.

Another length of walled-in climbing, then again corridors—four this time.

Troy's ribs ached; his breath came in heaving gasps. More and more often he had to pause to rest. But he was driven now by the need to gain the open air and the world he knew. How long that climb continued he could not have told, for at last he moved through a daze of fatigue, weaving and staggering from wall to wall on the ramp, no longer aware of any communication with the animals, or even if they were still with him. It seemed that the residue of terror that had sent him out of that cavern grew stronger instead of weaker as he went, until it blanketed out his normal reactions and whipped him on and on—

Then there was gray light—and cool air, fresh air—air that bore with it the burden of fine rain, but which cleansed him and fought the shadows in his mind. Troy reeled, caught at a block of masonry, dimly conscious that he was out in the open now and that he was done. With that crumbling wall as a prop to keep him from crashing on his face, he slid down and lay on his back, the soft steady rain pouring over his face and body, plastering his clothing to him.

"Danger!" That word rang in his head as a shout might have torn at his eardrums. Troy raised his head groggily. The rain was over. There was a patch of sunlight on the ground just beyond his hand. He shook his head, trying to wake up fully.

Then he heard more than that mental warning. He heard the sound made by a flitter hovering over a landing site in a cramped space. A flitter!

More by instinct than by any conscious move, Troy drew back against the wall that had given him partial

157

shelter, trying to locate the machine, which, by the sound, must be very close. Around him were the domes and walls of surface Ruhkarv. There could be only one reason why anyone had invaded this forbidden territory —they must have traced him here. And who were "they"? The patrollers, Zul—or the rangers on their usual duty of keeping the unauthorized out of this danger zone?

For the first time he looked about for the animals. And they were nowhere to be seen. Even the injured Sahiba had disappeared. Yet they had warned him mentally—or had they? Perhaps he was only still tuned in on some wave length of their intercommunication.

The sound of the flitter grew louder, and Troy tried to squeeze his bulk smaller in the shadow of the wall. He saw the flyer as it crossed between two domes. It was that of a ranger.

Troy crept backward, angling toward the mouth of the ramp. He discovered that the fact he might be the object of an air search removed a great deal of the nebulous distaste he had known in the depths. Then, to his astonishment, for he had felt very naked and plainly in sight, he watched the flitter keep straight on course and vanish behind the rise of another dome, the sound of its passing dying away in the distance. With a sigh of relief he sat up.

"Simba, Sahiba—" He pictured the cats in his mind, aimed his mental call.

"One comes."

Troy was not sure of the direction of that ambiguous answer.

"The flitter has gone." He tried to reassure the furred company, to summon one of them into sight.

158

"One comes." It was repeated. "One comes from the big man."

From the big man—Kyger! Zul?

"Where?" Troy pushed that effort at communication to the top pitch he could hold. For a long moment he feared they had cut their contact, refusing to answer. Then Shang frisked around the swell of the dome behind which the flitter had disappeared, showed himself to Troy, and was gone again.

With far less speed and agility the man followed that lead, crossing the space between wall and dome with care as to his path but as quickly as he could. Then, one hand braced against the side of the structure, the other gripping his stunner, he began a slow and, he hoped, a noiseless journey. He could hear the buzz of a few insects. But there were no birds here, no sign of life in this desolation that was the upper cover of Ruhkarv. And he caught no sign of the animals save that momentary glimpse of Shang.

Fourteen

Perhaps it was because his body was pressed so tightly to the masonry of the dome that Troy caught the first vibration, a faint tingle through blood and bone that was familiar, bringing with it a vague memory of darkness and suspense.

That throb grew faster, and it pulled, pulled against

his intelligence, against the need for caution, making Troy want to run toward its source.

He battled that impulse, holding to cover, but moving on with that hardly heard beat for his goal, that thrumming which registered on his nerves and muscles before it did on his eardrums. And along with his involuntary answer to that call, there came now another emotion—not his, but the animals'! A desperation—the hopeless fear of bound and helpless prisoners.

Tasting their fear, Troy guessed the truth. Somewhere ahead Zul was using the cylinder that had rested in Kyger's lifeless hands. And the animals, conditioned to answer its summons, were being drawn to their own end without any chance to fight for their freedom. Just as that cord within him, which was able to serve as a communicating link from their brains to his, was also responding—

Only he had not been conditioned—he could fight back! And Zul would lead him straight to where he wanted to go.

Troy ceased to resist, allowed his hidden compass to guide him. But, though he followed the line of that infernal piping, he still kept to cover.

Between two more domes, then into a space of open land with straight towers of rock outcrops. As soon as Troy was sure of his goal, he swung to the right, pulling out of the direct line of the piping, circling to bring up to the rear of the suspected ambush. Was Zul alone? So much depended upon that.

Troy reached the first of the rock outcrops, went in a half stoop to round it and thread a path of his own. The piping still continued, which meant that Zul had

160

not yet pulled the animals out of hiding. But, as Troy came to the tallest pillar in that broken land, it stopped abruptly, and then he knew that he must trade caution for speed.

His stunner ready, he whipped around the base of that tower to find the scene he had expected. Zul was there, and between his knees was the tube from Kyger's chambers. He had one hand still cupping its length. The other, with wrist steadied on the head of the cylinder, grasped a blaster. While facing him, crouching, snarling, betraying in their tense bodies their hatred and their fear—and helplessness—were the animals.

Troy snapped the stunner, aiming for the difficult point of that bony yellow wrist. A head target would have been best—but even as he blacked out under the bolt, Zul could still have triggered his blaster. Now the numbing beam struck the curled fingers with better success than Troy had dared to hope for. Zul cried out with the shock and surprise, his voice thinned by rocky echoes. The blaster spun from his deadened fingers. Grabbing for it with his other hand, he lost his hold on the tube.

When Troy thumbed for a second stunner shot, the release light did not spark. Charge exhausted! He sprang into the open, running for the blaster. Zul was down on his knees, his numbed hand folded up against his chest, the other within fingertip reach of the blaster grip. Troy swung a boot toe forward, kicked the blaster away from Zul but out of his own path also.

Zul was well-versed in rough-and-tumble. The hand that had been straining for the blaster grip struck out at Troy's ankle, fingers raked across his boot, sending him enough off balance to stagger a step or two beyond the smaller man. Horan brought up against one of the rock pillars with force enough to awaken the pain in his old bruises, and clawed about breathlessly just in time to face death.

Erupting from his half crouch, the blade of a knife glinting in the sun, Zul came at him. Troy knew his attack would end in the vicious up-cut that would finish the fight and him in one skilled stroke if he could not counter it. He was no knife fighter and Zul was.

But Zul's right hand was numbed and perhaps he was awkward with the left. There was only that one small chance. Troy swerved and struck for Zul's head with the barrel of the stunner. The jar of that blow getting home was followed by a thud against his own ribs, so sharp and painful as to bring a yelp of agony out of him.

Zul staggered against the rock, recoiled, and slumped to the ground. Troy, hands pressed to his side, needed the support of the pillar or he would have joined him. He looked down, expecting to see the hilt of the blade projecting from his flesh. But on the ground at his feet lay the knife snapped in two pieces, and there was a line of welling red on his arm above and below the strange wristlet he had brought out of Ruhkarv. Dazed, he watched the blood gather and drip, realizing tardily that a super-steel blade meeting that red band had been broken like a stick of dead wood and that, thanks to the bracelet, he was still alive.

Holding his arm pressed tightly to his side to slow the flow of blood, Troy stooped over Zul. The yellow man lay limply on the ground but he was still breathing.

"Behind you—"

Troy tried to turn, tripped on Zul's outflung arm,
162

and went to his knees, so saving his life, for he cowered just beyond the searing edge of a blaster beam. He coughed in the ozone stench of the discharge. Then, obeying the instinct of self-preservation, he rolled across the ground, sick with the torment of his side and arm, gaining cover behind another rock pillar. So Zul had at least one companion. And disarmed and wounded, Troy would now be hunted down, with all the advantages on the side of the hunter.

In his desire to hide, Troy knew of only one place—the depths of Ruhkarv. Its evil reputation might slow up pursuit, give him a breathing space. If he could only have reached the blaster he had stunned out of Zul's hand! But there was no chance to hunt for that now—not with a sniper ready to fry him if he ventured into the open.

"The depths," he thought fuzzily, trying to contact the animals, sure that they had scattered into hiding when he had broken Zul's spell-binding with the tube.

The tube! With that in Zula's or another's hands the fugitives had no chance at all. Troy looked about him a little widlly. There it lay—one end projecting beyond a stone. To leave that intact meant disaster. Horan hunted for a weapon—any kind of weapon.

He chose a stone block detached from a nearby dome, of a size to fit his hand. And he hurled it—to strike hard and true. Under its impact the tube cracked, the end shattered, past any repair, he trusted. Their luck had held—this far.

Then, his throbbing arm tight against his chest, Troy scuttled away, expecting every moment to see the flash of another blaster beam or feel his flesh crisp under the beam he did not see.

Somehow he made it, falling rather than running into the open mouth of the ramp up which they had come hours before with such hope. And that beam he had been anticipating struck as he fell and rolled down the inside slope. He saw the brilliant, eye-searing flash and heard the crackle as it lapped stone. Then he was beyond its reach, only aware that somehow he was still alive, if badly battered.

Would his tracker come boldly on? Troy tried to listen. He could not see well; his eyes were still dazzled by the last shot. What he did hear was the return of the flitter, or else another flyer. And that might have provided a signal of sorts, for dark shapes flowed over the edge of the ramp above, visible only for a second or two against the circle of the daylight. The animals were on their way to join him.

Together they retired to the first level of corridors and there paused. There was no sound from above. Had the rangers' scout seen the activity in the ruins and landed to investigate? Troy knew that he had left Zul partially stunned but still able to join the chase. If he only had the blaster that the other had dropped in their first encounter—

"It is here."

Sahiba! Troy dared for an instant to snap on the atom torch. The gray-blue cat, her splinted leg held at an awkward angle, was half lying, half sitting, close to him, and next to her was her mate. And in front of Simba rested the weapon Troy had longed for. He caught it up, feeling the dampness of the cat's mouth-carry on the slender barrel, checking the charge. That was less than a third expended. Now he could defend them.

"They come." That was Sargon.

"How many?" Troy demanded.

"One—there are others—still above—"

One. Zul, or the unseen with the blaster? Troy eyed the corridors issuing from the ramp, then flashed off his torch. To venture blindly along any of those might be to lose oneself entirely. Better the dangers he knew than a new host, especially with the hunt behind, for Troy was certain that Zul was not going to give up. And he tried to plan ahead. Perhaps in that tangled jungle below he could find the means of turning tables on the other.

There was the problem of water and food. His bag of supplies had been abandoned in the open. But there was water below, and perhaps food, if he was not dainty. He knew that the animals had found edible prey in the fungoid cavern.

"Down!" He picked up Sahiba, unsealing the front of his tunic and settling the cat into an improvised carrying bag, which left his good arm free. The cuts on his left forearm had stopped bleeding, but he feared to use it freely lest they begin to ooze again.

Though no sounds save his own breathing, the faint scurrying that marked the going of the animals, and the thin click of his boots reached his ears, Troy's scouts assured him that the pursuit was still in progress as they retreated to the level of the next set of corridors and on back to the haunted wilderness cavern. He went without the torch, feeling his way, and now the pallid seep of light below marked their goal.

When he dropped from the foot of the ramp, Troy discovered the weird daylight was again in effect. Perhaps it was true sunlight beamed through some unknown process of Ruhkarv's builders into this hollow. There was a line of clouds discharging their burden of rain, and Troy dodged to a dry space beyond. He came against the rock wall where a filament of gray-white stuff clung, and his shoulder brushed against it—to adhere so that he had to jerk to free himself.

That was one of the web cords—strung all the way from the opening—which had made a fatal trap for Fauklow's man.

With the glimmering of an idea, Troy examined the length carefully. He discovered that it was not plastered to the stone surface along its entire side, as he had first feared, but attached at intervals by thicker portions. Thrusting his blaster into his belt, he pried between two of those buttons and, either because the cord was old or because it had never been meant to grip too tightly except at those points, he freed a loop.

Troy worked fast. There were other cords, some thinner, one or two as thick, and he moved them with caution, picking the suckers away from the wall. The outer sides were adhesive in the extreme. Sometimes the ends he loosened flopped and became irretrievably glued together before he could prevent their touching.

But even laboring one-handed he had a net of sorts, though very crude and far from the perfect mesh he had seen set over two of the cavern entrances. With infinite care he spread his trap at the foot of the ramp before the chopped-out trail that marked their former trip through the jungle. Why he had been allowed time enough to finish the job he did not know. But the animals posted on the ramp had not given the alarm.

At Troy's signal they leaped free of the tangle now lightly covered with dust and trampled leaves. To the
166

man's eye the net was well hidden, and he hoped his pursuers would be as blind. Then they took cover, the animals—except Sahiba—under the fringe of vegetation, Troy and Sahiba in the pocket between wall and ramp.

They had set the trap. But was a trap any good without bait? There had been no sight or sound of the enemy for more than an hour. Had the other—or others—stopped to explore the level corridors?

Man had only a scant portion of the patience of the four-footed hunters, as Troy was to discover. His skin itched; his side and arm throbbed. Hunger and thirst clawed at his insides. A hundred minor irritations of which he would not have ordinarily been conscious arose to the point of torment. The sinister vegetation that had repelled him earlier now beckoned with a promise of food and water—somewhere—somehow—

And under that physical discomfort lay the malaise of spirit that had troubled him before when night had caught him in this place—the suggestion that there were unseen terrors here worse than any danger he could face body to body, weapon to weapon.

Troy battled discomfort, vague fears, held himself taut, hoping his forlorn hope would work. But how long he could keep this watch he did not know. A trap—but a trap needed bait.

A bush trembled. Shang sprang from its crown onto the ramp. He stood so for a moment, his prehensile tail curled up in a question mark, hindquarters up slope, his round head atilt as he looked down at Troy.

"No." The man protested. The kinkajou could move fast, Troy would bear witness to that, but not fast enough to escape a blaster bolt.

But the animal did not heed him. Out of reach, the

kinkajou was now out of sight as well, up the ramp. The bait had been provided.

Sahiba shifted her weight inside his tunic, making Troy catch his breath as one of her hind paws scraped his tender ribs.

"One comes?" he asked hopefully.

His less able sense of contact caught again the fringe of their joint concentration, the filament that must unite them to Shang up there in the danger of the higher levels. And Troy, impatient, knew that he could not badger them with questions now.

Time crept. Once more dusk was growing in the jungle, patch of shadow united with patch of shadow, and did not retreat but became solid.

"One comes!" Sahiba dug the claws of her good forepaw into Troy's flesh, jerking him out of a nod. He drew the blaster, took the cat out of his tunic, and set her in safety behind him.

A scurry on the ramp. Shang flew through the air from the stone to the bushes. And now—louder—the click of shod feet—human feet.

Above, a flicker of light—gone almost as instantly as Troy had sighted it. An atom torch snapped on and off again? He was sure that the newcomer must have seen the thin light of the cavern and would now proceed guided by that alone.

"Zul?" He beamed that at Shang.

"No."

If not Zul, then it must be that unknown who had sniped with the blaster. Troy readied his own weapon. Whether he could burn down another human being, even when fighting for his life, he was not sure. The struggles in the Dipple had always been man to man,

168

ist and foot. And a knife was an accepted combat arm
nywhere on Korwar, in fact across the stellar lanes.
But this thing in his hand—he did not know, though
he was very sure no such scruples would check the
ther.

The click of boots was still. Had the other halted—or
urned back?

"No!" A reply concentrated in force from the animals.

Then it was stealth. Troy crouched, steadied his
laster hand against the wall. Yet for all his long
eriod of waiting he was not quite prepared for the
udden spring from the head of the ramp.

His own slight movement might have spiked that
ttack and almost spoiled his plan. But Troy had
lanted the net well. The man fell short and his land-
ng was not clean. He went to his hands and knees, to
e enmeshed in the sticky ropes, which, as he rolled
nd fought, only tied the more tightly about his body.

Troy stood away from the wall. He would not be
orced to fire after all. The other was doing a good job
f making himself a prisoner.

"Another—"

The warning startled Troy out of his absorption in
he struggle. Simba advanced into the open, avoiding
he flopping captive, to stand at the foot of the ramp
ooking up.

Then a blaster bolt crackled—striking not for Troy,
s he had expected, but at the writhing figure on the
round, close enough to singe some of the cords so
hat they flaked away from smoldering clothing. The
ound man gave a mighty heave and rolled, as a
econd bolt burned the soil where he had lain and cut
 blackened slash into the jungle.

And by that flash Troy saw the hide tunic the othe wore. The trapped man was not Zul but one of th rangers. Horan snapped an answering bolt recklessl' up the ramp. There was a cry and a figure staggere into view, slipped, rolled to the cavern floor. When did not stir again, Troy went to the ranger.

"I thought I might find you here, Horan."

He was looking down at Rerne. And his first im pulse to free the other died. Once he had almost turne to this man for help. Now all the instincts of th hunted brought back his long-seated suspicions. H might well have as good a reason to fear Rerne as h did Zul. Not that the ranger would blast him withou warning, but the Clans had their own laws and thos laws were obeyed in the Wild. Troy did not sheath the blaster, but over its barrel he regarded the Hunte narrowly.

"Do not be a fool." Rerne had stopped struggling but he was trying to raise his head and shoulder from the ground. "You are being hunted."

"I know," Troy interrupted. "You are here—"

Rerne frowned. "You have more after you than Cla rangers, boy. Including some who want you dead, no alive. Ha—"

His gaze swept from Troy to a point nearer groun level. Troy follow the path of his eyes. Shang, Simba Sargon, and Sheba had materialized in their usua noiseless fashion, were seated at their ease inspectin Rerne with that measuring stare Troy could still fin disconcerting when it was turned in his directior Sahiba came limping from the place where he had let her for safety.

"So—" Rerne returned the steady-eyed regard of the animals, his expression eager. "These are the present most-wanted criminals of Korwar."

Fifteen

Most wanted, maybe,"—Troy's voice was soft, cold, one he had never used before to any man outside the Dipple—"but not criminals, Rerne." No more subservient "Hunter" or "Gentle Homo." This was not Tikil but a place into which the men of Tikil feared to go, and he was no longer a weaponless city laborer but one of a company who were ready to fight for what the Dipple had never held—freedom.

"You know how they served Kyger?" Rerne asked almost casually.

"I know."

"But you could not have been a part of that—or could you?" That last portion of the question might be one Rerne was asking himself—had been asking himself—for some time. He was studying Troy with a stare almost as unblinking as that Simba could turn upon one.

"No, I was not a part of Kyger's schemes, whatever those were. And I did not kill him—if you have any doubts about that. But neither are we criminals."

"We?"

Troy took a step backward to join the half circle of animals. They stood together now, presenting a united front to the ranger. Rerne nodded.

"I see, it is indeed 'we'."

"And what do you propose to do about it?" Troy challenged.

"It is not what I propose to do, Horan. We shall all probably die unless we can work together to find a safe way out of here." But he sounded calm enough. "You are being hunted by more than just Clan rangers —in fact, the rangers could be the least of your worries. And it seems that the order is out to blast before asking questions—blast on sight."

"Your orders?" Troy brought up his own weapon.

"Hardly. And when they hear about it, the Clan shall take steps. That I promise you." There was ice in that, and Troy, noting the narrowing of the other's eyes, the slight twist of his lips, estimated the quality of the anger this man held under rigid control. "It is easy to eliminate a fugitive and afterwards swear that his death was all an unfortunate mistake—the game our friend over there was trying to play." He jerked his head toward the body at the foot of the ramp. "You have one chance in a thousand of escaping one or another of the packs after you now or—" He was summarily interrupted.

"One comes." Simba padded to the foot of the ramp again.

Troy hesitated. He could leave Rerne where he was, neatly packaged, for either the ranger's own men or someone else to discover—and melt back into the jungle, eventually seeking the yet lower level of the fungoid cavern, retracing their whole journey through

172

Ruhkarv. Or he could make a stand here and fight.

Rerne's eyes traveled from cat to man and back again. "We are about to entertain another visitor?"

"We?" This time it was Troy who accented the pronoun.

"It could not be my men coming now."

And Troy believed him. That meant it was truly the enemy.

"You have a choice," Rerne pointed out. "Take to the bush over there and they will have a difficult time beating you out of it—"

"And you?"

"Since you can name me one of your pursuers, should that matter?" There was a grim lightness in that.

"The other one tried to burn you."

"As I said, they are working on the principle that accidents will happen and a dead man one has to explain is better than a live witness who can explain for himself."

Troy made the only possible choice. Hooking his fingers in the nearest loop of the cords about the ranger, he jerked the man under the overhang of the ramp. There was no time now to try to free Rerne, even if he were yet sure he wanted to. But he knew he could not leave the other helpless to take a blasting from Zul or one of Zul's crowd.

"Zul?" he asked Simba.

"Zul," the cat replied with sure authority.

There was no time either in which to rig another trap, and Troy was sure the other came armed. Nor could he count on another shot as lucky as the one that had brought down the earlier assailant. Now he squatted beside Rerne, hoping for a workable ambush.

"Get me loose!" The ranger's shoulders heaved as he worked his muscles against the cords of the webbing.

"Nothing will cut those except heat," Troy told him absently, most of his attention on what might be happening up ramp.

"What is this stuff?" Rerne demanded, his voice a whisper.

"Part of a web—taken from the wall over there." Troy nodded to the stretch of rock where strips of cord and thread still hung in tatters. Rerne gave a small gasp and was silent.

The light was fading steadily into a dark that had none of the quality of the upper-surface night. Troy remembered his first stay in this place, his belief that the jungle had its own brand of very dangerous life. There was one place free of that growth—the section of pavement where the recaller stood. And as long as that machine was deadened—

If Zul did not come soon, should they try to reach that? Troy seesawed between one plan and the other. Wait here for Zul and try to shoot as soon as he appeared on the ramp, when he could not be too sure of his aim in the failing light? Or free Rerne's legs and bundle the ranger along to that haunted spot beside the recaller with the warning of that shriveled, long-dead thing set up to stare at them through the night hours?

"Zul?" Again he asked that of those who were quicker than he to know whether danger ran or crept toward them now.

Simba again answered, but this time with a puzzled shading to his mind speech. "Zul begins to fear—"

"Us?" Troy could hardly believe that. He knew well

that Zul had had no fear when they had fought above, that Zul looked upon the animals as creatures he could control, could entice helpless to their deaths. What and why did he fear now? Or was it the presence of Rerne that was a restraining factor? Could Troy somehow use the Hunter to bargain with?

"Zul fears what he cannot see," Simba reported, still that puzzlement coloring his reply.

For a moment Simba's report fed Troy's own latent uneasiness. With the dusk closing in about them and the only too clearly remembered picture of the captive in the web at the back of his mind, he thought he knew what could plague a man, eating at his nerves until he had to get out of this hidden pocket within Ruhkarv. But Zul had not been here; he could not know of the web, or the recaller, or guess at what might have been summoned and now, according to the animals, still hovered just beyond the bonds of living consciousness. Why did Zul fear?

"He does not see," Sahiba cut in, "not with his eyes—only with his far thoughts. But he is a kind who feels trouble before him."

"He is able to speak to you then?"

"No." That was Sargon. "Not without the aid of the thing-which-calls. But Zul sees many shadows now and each holds an enemy." The fox trotted out of hiding, made a detour about the body of the dead man, and advanced a foot or so up the ramp, surveying the gloom above. "He wishes to come, yet his fears hold him back."

And did Zul have a right to fear? Troy watched the now night-disguised splotch of the jungle. And he knew that he could no longer plan to pass through even a fringe of it, much less intrude upon that open space about the recaller. It was as if that thing, which lurked—not alive, yet not wholly in the dead past either—sucked vitality from the dark, made itself substance that could not be seen with the eyes, but which could be sensed by that other thing inside one, the thing that allowed him to communicate with the animals.

"What is it?" Rerne, too, his shoulders braced against the rock wall, was staring into that mass of vegetation. "What walks there?"

"Nothing alive—I hope." Troy went down on one knee, sparked his blaster on low power, and touched lightly the coils of webbing still encircling the other's legs. The strands shriveled and were gone.

"Nothing alive?" Rerne repeated questioningly.

"The recaller Fauklow brought is out there. Your machine muted it, but the power is still on—blanketed. They tell me that what it summoned is still partly in this dimension."

"What! And I take it that our friend above is reluctant to descend into what may prove to be a dragon's jaws?"

Troy sat back on his heels. Had Rerne been able to tune in on that conversation between Troy and the animals? But he was certain that the animals would have known of such eavesdropping and would have warned him.

"You communicate with the animals somehow," Rerne continued. "And now you suspect that I can also."

Troy nodded.

"Mental contact." That was a stated fact, not a
176

question. "No, I have been guessing only. And this I do know, Zul is of unusual stock. Most of us now are a mingling of many races, the result of centuries of stellar colonization. He is a primitive out of Terra—pure Bushman—a race of hunters and desert dwellers with an inborn instinct for the Wild such as few others have today. And such primitives keep senses we have lost. If he sniffs your demon, then I do not think that mere duty will drive him down. Rather he will comfort his conscience with the belief that the demon will account for us—if he sits over the exit and so locks us in. And at that, I can almost find myself agreeing with such reasoning."

Rerne moved his shoulders again, straining at the remaining cords. "This is not a place in which I would choose to spend the night," he confessed, and there was no light touch to those words.

"You were here when Fauklow was found?"

"Not here. We did not know this particular beauty spot existed. After what we saw aloft there was no nonsense about exploring below ground. We thought we had accounted for the recaller, though. That must be seen to. That is, if I ever get out of here to report it."

"He can wait up there a long time—pick us off easily if we try to pass." Troy wondered if now was the time to reveal the alternate route to the surface. Without food and water—no, he was not sure they could make it back the longer way around.

"Yes, any one of those level corridors would make him a good cover for ambush. But if we cannot get up, we can bring help from the surface to take him in the rear." Again Rerne tried to flex his upper arms. "If

177

you will just loose me the rest of the way, Horan, I can bring in reinforcements."

"No." Troy's dissent was flat and quick.

"Why?" Rerne did not sound angry, merely interested.

"We are criminals—remember?"

"Where there is a common enemy there can be a truce. In the Wild I do have some small authority."

Troy considered that. Trust was a rare commodity in the Dipple. If he gave his now to this man, as he was so greatly tempted to do, he would be putting a weapon in Rerne's hands just as surely as if he were to hand over the blaster. And again his suspicion warred with his desire to believe in the other.

"A truce, until we are out of here," Rerne suggested. "I am willing to swear knife oath if you wish."

Troy shook his head. "Your word, no oaths—if I accept." He paid that much tribute openly to the ranger. "Truce and a head start for me, with them."

"The chase will be up again," Rerne warned. "You have no chance with the Clans out to quarter the field. Better surrender and let the law decide."

"The law?" Troy laughed harshly. "Which law, Hunter—Clan right, patrollers' code, or Zul's extermination policy? I know we are fair game. No, give me your promise that we can have a start of at least half a day."

"That is freely yours, for what you can make of it, which I am afraid will be very little."

"We shall take our chances." Troy applied heat to the other's remaining bonds.

"Always *we*. Why, Horan?" Rerne rubbed his wrists.

"Men have used animals as tools," Troy said slowly,
178

trying to fit into words something he did not wholly understand himself. "Now some men, somewhere, have made better tools, tools so good they can turn and cut the maker. But that is not the fault of the tools—that they are no longer tools but—"

"Perhaps companions?" Rerne ended for him, his fingers still stroking his ridged flesh, but his eyes very intent on Troy.

"How did you know?" the younger man was startled into demanding.

"Let us say that I am also a workman who can admire fine tools, even when they have ceased, as you point out, to be any longer tools."

Troy grasped at that hint of sympathy. "You understand—"

"Only too well. Most of our breed want tools, not companions. And the age-old fear of man, that he will lose his supremacy, will bring all the hawks and hunters of the galaxy down on your trail, Horan. Do not expect any aid from your own species when it is threatened by powers it cannot and does not want to understand. But you will have your truce—and your head start—and what you do with them is up to you. Now, let us see what we can do about getting a clear road out of here before what prowls over there takes a fancy to come out." Rerne waved a hand toward the jungle.

He slipped a small object from a loop on his belt. On its surface was a tiny dial he set with care, holding it into the beam of an atom torch. Then he smiled at Troy.

"Broadcaster. It is beamed for a ranger aid call, and I have alternated that with a warning code, so they

179

will not head blindly into any ambush of Zul's. He may have another man with him, possibly two. We know that he went to the Guild in Tikil before he coasted in here. I think he hired blaster men."

"Then he must have robbed Kyger's. He would not have credits enough on his own to pay blaster man prices to the Thieves' Guild."

"Did you ever think that perhaps Kyger was not the top man of his organization on Korwar?" returned Rerne. "If he was not, then it is up to that head to close down the whole enterprise as quickly and with as little fuss as possible. You have already been posted in Tikil as a murderer who has stolen valuable animals. Someone issued that complaint."

"I thought that would happen." Troy governed his dismay speedily. Posted as a murderer! Which meant that even the city patrollers could shoot first and ask troublesome questions after. Only this was the Wild, not Tikil, and he thought he had an advantage over that set of trackers here.

"You say that you did not kill him?"

"I found him dead." Swiftly Troy outlined the events before his escape from the shop and from Tikil that night.

"That account I can readily believe. Kyger had some odd acquaintances and had stepped hard on the wrong toes," Rerne commented obscurely, "apart from these other activities. And do you realize that I can supply you with an alibi? At the time Kyger died you were with Rogarkil and me."

"Did you say that to the patrollers?" Troy's throat felt tight. If that was the truth, why had Rerne not cleared him?

"Not so far—"

"You wanted a bargaining point to use with me?" Troy demanded. That seesaw of belief, then suspicion, within him swung once more to the chilling side.

"Perhaps."

"I am not interested. I will take what I have." Troy was cooling rapidly. He was sure Rerne would keep his word to the strict letter of his promise. But why the ranger had revealed this other matter—that he could clear Troy with the law of the city but had not done so—remained a mystery. It smelled of the desire to push Horan into some pattern of Clan devising, just as he and the other had obliquely suggested at that café meeting. And having tasted freedom, Troy was not minded to walk again another's road.

"As you wish." Rerne neither urged nor explained. He raised the miniature com unit to his ear, listened for a moment, and then nodded.

"They are coming, have laid down a haze ahead—as far as the levels. Should not be long before that reaches Zul."

So the rangers were using that most up-to-date subduing weapon—and one Zul, Troy was certain, was not armored against.

"Will they arrest Zul?"

Rerne glanced at him. "Is that what you wish?"

"Why not?"

"There is no reason to believe that Zul is top man. He was wholly Kyger's subordinate, not the other way around. Zul, left free, could lead someone to his employer."

"If that trailer had time—and the inclination," snapped Troy. "Just a present I have more important

181

things—" He paused. Rerne was right in a way. To trace Zul's contacts to their sources. If it were not for the animals, he would like to do just that. But he must make the best use of his truce, and he could not waste time on Zul. "Your move, if you wish," he suggested.

Rerne was holding the broadcaster to his ear again. "Our move is up." He gestured to the ramp.

"Zul?"

"No sign of him. But there is a Guildsman sleeping sweetly at the second level. They have collected him for the patrollers. Let Zul believe that he has made a safe escape in his hiding place. He will sleep off the haze and he can be watched later."

So Rerne was going to investigate Zul? Though what he would make of more exact knowledge, except to use it as a lever for some Clan dispute with the authorities in Tikil, Troy did not see. He gathered up Sahiba, motioned Rerne to precede them.

"I have a blaster. You have granted me a truce. Maybe some of the rest up there will not be so generous."

Rerene smiled. "It pays to be cautious. But I think you will find I speak for the rangers. Up it is."

To Troy the climb was as long and exhausting as had been the descent of the winding way in the well. There was no one waiting at the first level of corridors. On and up, Simba and Sargon forging a little ahead, a twin pair of scouts Troy was sure no human being could equal. Shang was on his shoulder, Sheba beside him. None of the animals paid any attention to Rerne outwardly, but Troy knew they kept an expert watch on the ranger.

They passed the second level. Ahead lay the open.

Troy pushed his weary brain to plan action beyond that point. He could not hope that he would have any chance at mechanical transport; his bargain did not reach that far. But the barrier about Ruhkarv must have been lowered to let the searchers in, so they could leave this scar on foot. Tired as he was, without supplies, he did not see how they would be able to cover much ground. But even if they could reach the fringe of forest lands, the animals could escape. Then he would take his chances with the men.

"Men waiting," Simba warned.

Well, that was to be expected—Rerne's men.

"Not enemies," Troy replied.

"We have you covered! Drop your blaster!"

Troy spun halfway around as he caught a glimpse of a uniformed shoulder, a hand holding a blaster. His arm, still stiff from the cut, went up and his fingers gripped Rerne, pulling the other to him as a shield. He heard a gasp from the ranger and an exclamation of anger.

"So this is the worth of a Clansman's word!" Troy spat. "Would your knife oath have held any better?" Then he raised his voice to reach the others. "We got out—this Hunter lord with us. Any attempted burndown and he roasts too!"

Rerne offered no resistance as Troy propelled him ahead into the open. There was a muttering behind but no bolt to shatter the gloom.

Sixteen

Rerne was oddly silent; he had made no reply to Troy's accusation. That bothered the younger man; he wanted an explanation, to know that the other had not purposely led him into a trap. Now that he had a moment to think, he believed that scrap of uniform so briefly glimpsed had not been ranger dress.

"Men here—" Again that alert from the animals.

Troy, holding the unresisting Rerne to him, stood—back to the dome wall—surveying the scene. He could see those others waiting—and they were unmistakably rangers, the hunting dress blending into the earth color of the ruins. A little beyond was what he had not dared to hope for—a flitter!

"Tell your men," he said harshly to his prisoner, "to stand away from the flitter—now!"

"Leave the flitter," Rerne repeated obediently, his voice as toneless as that of a com robot. His features were set and hard, and Troy sensed his rage.

The rangers moved. When they were well away from the flyer, Troy began a crablike journey in its direction, keeping Rerne between him and the Clan men, knowing the animals were well ahead of him. Then he was at his goal, his hand on the cabin door.

His anger and fear driving him, Troy swung the blaster, laid the barrel against Rerne's head. The Hunter gasped, his knees buckled, and he dropped to the ground. Troy scrambled into the flyer, knocked down the rise lever. They climbed in a jump, which shook him across the control board and made Sahiba yowl in protest as she was scraped against that obstruction. But they were safe for the moment; he was sure the zoom had lifted them out of range of blaster fire. Free and in a flitter.

He twirled the journey dial to the east, knowing that the flyer, without any tending from him, would keep straight for the heart of the Wild. They would be after him surely. But unless they had another flitter at Ruhkarv, there would be precious time lost until they could summon one, and time was all he dared hope to gain now.

Troy's eyes were fixed unseeingly on the night sky that held them. Food—water—shelter—His mind felt as sapped of energy as his body. He could not think properly. Of only one thing was he sure: a stubborn determination to set down the flyer somewhere in the Wild where the animals could take to the country for their own concealment.

"It is well." That was Simba. "Good hunting here. Men cannot shake us out of these lands."

"There is still Zul," Troy warned sluggishly.

"There is still Zul," Simba agreed. "But let Zul follow us before we lay a trap for his feet."

Troy must have slept. He aroused with light in his eyes, sat up groggily, for a moment unable to remember where he was. Then the golden sky of morning, patterned with the clouds of fair weather, recalled the immediate past. Under him the flitter rode steadily on the course he had set—eastward.

He looked down through the bubble, expecting to see the rolling plains he had hoped to find. They spread beneath him right enough, only ahead was a distant smudge of darker vegetation, the sign of a forest or more broken ground. They must have passed over a large section of the open territory during the night and were leagues deep into the reserve, farther than the Tikil hunting parties ever went. Troy rubbed his eyes, began to think again.

The only way they could be traced now was by the flitter. Suppose he were to land by the edge of that distant wood and then send the flyer off on remote control—back to the west? One way of confusing the pursuit.

But, as he reached for the controls, to take the flyer back under manual pilotage again, his time had run out. The flitter plunged crazily, caught in the side sweep of a traction beam. Troy gave one startled look to the rear, saw another flyer boring down his track.

Perhaps a more skilled pilot could have done better. His evasive swings only kept him out of the direct core of the beam the other had trained upon his craft. He set the air speed to the top notch, striving to reach the wood before the other pinned him squarely.

At last Troy set down, felt the wheels of the flitter catch and tear through the long grass. But that grass could cover his passengers' escape. He slewed the flyer about, broadside to the first tongue of woods cover. Opening the door of the cabin before they bumped to a complete halt, he gave his last command to the animals: "Out and hide!"

Sahiba he set down himself, saw her limp into a tangle of grass with her mate, the foxes and the kinkajou already gone. Then Troy sent the flyer on, scuttling along the ground as far and as fast from the point where he had dropped his live cargo as he could get.

The flitter rocked, half lifted from the ground. Now he was pinned to his seat, helpless, unable to raise as much as a finger from the controls. They had a pinner beam on him, and he was a captive forced to wait for the arrival of his pursuer.

Unable to as much as turn his head, Troy sat sweating out the minutes of that wait. At least they wanted to take him prisoner, not just blast him out of the air as they might have done. Whether this was good or bad he had yet to learn. And whether his captors were rangers, patrollers, or Zul's ambiguous force he would know shortly.

The cabin door was pulled open. Though he could not turn his head, Troy rolled his eyes to the right far enough to see that the man who had thrust head and shoulders into that confined space was not wearing the hide forest dress of the Clans, not the uniform of a patroller. Zul's party—?

Paying little or no attention to the helpless prisoner before the controls, the other searched the floor, squeezed behind the seat to survey the storage space. Undoubtedly he was looking for the animals. And, guessing that, Troy's spirits rose a small fraction. They had either not noted his brief pause by the tongue of woodland, or they had not understood the reason for it. They had expected to find not one but six helpless in the flitter.

The man backed out of the door. "Not here." Troy heard his call.

187

Though he knew he could not fight the tension bands of a pinner, Troy strove to move just his hand. The blaster butt was a painful knob against his chest, held upright by his belt. If he could only close his fingers about that, the man by the door and the one he reported to—he could turn tables on both of them. But, though blood throbbed in his temples from his efforts, he was held motionless and unable to resist any attack the others chose to make.

His eyes began to ache with the strain of trying to keep watch on the door of the cabin. But he did not have too long to wait. Zul, his yellow face a mask of pure and unshielded malignancy, took the place of his hireling there. As the other had done, he searched the floor of the machine, apparently unwilling or unable to accept that first report. Then he looked directly at Troy.

"They are gone!" He said that flatly.

At least vocal cords and throat muscles were not governed by the pinner. Troy was able to answer. "Where you will not find them."

Zul did not reply to that. Withdrawing from the cabin, he gave a low-voiced order. After a moment the door beside Troy was opened, and his disobedient muscles could not save him from falling through it, dropping to the ground on his face.

But the fall had removed him from the direct line of the pinner, and now he was free to move as the others, protected by countercharge buttons, had moved within the machine. He tried to get to his knees but he was not quick enough. A sharp pain burst at the nape of his neck, and he sprawled forward again, into the trampled grass of the plains.

Troy roused to utter darkness, a black that was frightening with its suggestion of blindness. And as he tried to raise his hand to his eyes, he made the discovery that he was bound, this time by no pinner but by very real cords, which chafed his wrists, drew hard loops about his ankles. A moment's experimentation informed him that it was no easier to loosen those than it had been to fight the beam. And he also learned that the dark came from an efficient and bewildering blindfold.

Whatever the intentions of his captors, they wanted to keep him alive for the present—and in reasonably good shape. Having made sure of his status as a wrapped package, Troy tried to figure out where he now was. The vibration, the small rough jolts of a swift air flight, were transmitted to his body through the surface of which he lay. His legs were curled behind him in a manner to stiffen muscles with cramp if he did not change position, and he could not. So Troy guessed that he now lay in the storage compartment of a flitter, in either the one in which he had made the dash from Ruhkarv, or the one in which Zul had tracked him.

And with Zul in command of that party, Troy thought that they must now be headed back toward Tikil— Tikil and perhaps the man who gave the orders now that Kyger was dead. The animals— They had expected to find them in the flitter. After they had stunned him had they discovered the animals? With nothing to bring them out of the woodland as Zul had drawn them with the summoner, Troy doubted that any of those who held him prisoner could have picked up the four-footed fugitives.

He tested his hope by trying to reach one of the animals with the mind touch. There was no response; he apparently had no fellow captives. Nor could he hear anything except the normal noises of a competently piloted flitter going at top legal speed—which meant they were flying high.

He had no way of telling how long he had been unconscious. But his middle was a hollow ache of hunger, and the thirst drying his throat was an additional pain; it was hard to remember now just when he had eaten last, harder yet to think back to a full drink of water. And these torments, added to the discomfort of his present position, spoiled his efforts to plan clearly, to try to speculate concerning what lay ahead of him at the end of this journey.

Troy wriggled, trying to work his legs straighter, then became aware of a change in the tempo of their flight. The pilot was cutting air speed, with a jerk that shook the flyer every time they dropped a notch —which argued the need for saving time. They must be ready to drop into a lower lane—could they be approaching Tikil?

Lying in his cramped curl, Troy tried to sort out the few impressions he could gather through the vibration of the flyer, the difference in small sounds. Yes, they were definitely dropping to a lower lane. Then he caught the whistle of a patroller flitter.

Troy tensed. Was this flyer being overhauled by the law?

But if the pilot had been questioned, he had been able to give the right signal answer, for there was no change in the beat of the engine—they had not been ordered to set down. However, the speed decreased
190

another notch. They were now traveling at the placid rate required for a low city lane, one used preparatory to landing.

Landing where? Troy's whole body ached now with the strain of trying to evaluate what he heard and felt. The swoop of the flitter he had been expecting. Then came the slight bound of a too-quick wheel touch, and the engine was snapped off.

Play dead, Troy thought. Let them haul him about as if he were still unconscious until he learned what he could. He forced his muscles to relax as well as he was able.

Air blew through the flitter. He heard the scrape of boots. Then another panel was opened only a few inches beyond his head. Hands, hooked in his armpits, jerked him roughly backward so that his legs hit the pavement. Grunting, the man who had unloaded him continued to drag Troy along.

But the air was providing the blindfolded prisoner with a clue to his whereabouts. Only one place had ever held that particular combination of strong odors —the courtyard of Kyger's shop. He was back to where he had started from days before.

He thudded to the ground, dropped by his guard, then heard the faint squeak of a panel door. Once more hands hooked under him and he was manhandled along. Again his nose supplied a destination. This was the storeroom off the courtyard. Troy was allowed to fall unceremoniously, his head and shoulders against a bag of grain, so that he was half sitting. He made his head loll forward in what he hoped was a convincing display of unconsciousness.

But if this convinced his captors, they were no longer

willing to let him remain unaware of his plight. Out of nowhere the flat of a palm smacked one cheek, snapping his head back against the bag. And a second stinging slap shook him equally as much.

"What—?" He did not need to counterfeit that dazed query.

"Wake up, Dippleman!" That was Zul. Yet Troy was sure the small man did not have the strength to drag him here. There must be at least two of them beside him in the storeroom.

"What—?" Troy began again.

"Use your mouth for this."

A hard metal edge was thrust against his lips with force enough to pinch flesh painfully against his teeth, and then he almost choked as a substance that was neither liquid nor solid but more nearly a thick soup filled his mouth and he had to swallow, a portion trickling out greasily over his chin. It had a bitter taste, but he could not struggle against their force-feeding methods, and about a cupful of it burned down his throat into his stomach.

"Will that hold?" someone, he thought it was Zul, asked.

"Never failed yet," returned a stranger briskly. "He'll be as frisky as one of those Dandle pups of yours about five hours from now. That's what you want, is it not? Up until then you can leave him here with all the doors wide open and he will not get lost. We know our job, Citizen."

Troy's head flopped forward on his chest once more as the other released his grip. There was no need to sham helplessness. Spreading outward from that warmth in his stomach was a numbness that attacked
192

muscles and nerves; he was completely unable to move. One of the notorious drugs used by the Guild. But, Troy thought dimly, that made this a highly expensive job—to include scientific drugging would put the price in the upper credit brackets. And where had Zul managed to lay his hands on that kind of funds—and the proper connections?

The numbness that had first affected his body now reached his mind. There was a dreamy lassitude in which nothing mattered. He lay quietly, drifting along on a softly swaying cloud that spiraled up lazily higher than any flitter could climb—

Cold—very cold— The cold centered in his head—no, in his mouth. Troy swallowed convulsively and the cold was in his throat—his middle—

"Thought you said he would be ready—" Words, the very sound of which jarred in his head.

"Does not usually work this way—unless he had an empty stomach to begin with." More words—protesting —hurting his head.

The cold spread outward, up through his shoulders, down his thighs, into his arms, hands, fingers, legs, and toes—a cold that bit, though he was unable to shiver.

"Get some sub-four into him now!" The order was rapped out in a louder tone.

More liquid splashed into his mouth, to dribble out again because he had no control over slack lips. Then his mouth was refilled, a palm held with brutal force over his lips, and he swallowed. The taste this time was sweet, cloying. But it drove out the ice as it went down him, bringing a glow, a feeling of returning energy and fitness, which was like a raw life force

193

being pumped into his veins to supply new vigor for his body.

"That does it." The hand that had been over his lips slipped down to rest on the pulse in his throat, then farther, inside his tunic, to touch directly over his heart. "He is coming around all right. He will be ripe and ready when you want him."

The fatigue, the hunger, the thirst of which Troy had been so conscious were gone. He was fully alert, not only physically but mentally, with an added fillip of rising self-confidence—though he mistrusted the latter, for that emotion might be born of the succession of drugs they had forced into him. A haffer addict, for example, simply did not believe that failure of any of his projects was possible. Had they pumped him full of something that would make him as amenable to their will or wills as the animals had been to Kyger's summoning tube?

However, for the moment they left him. His nose told Troy he was still in the storeroom of the shop, the bag of grain propping his shoulders. Beyond that there was little that hearing, touch, or smell could add. Time had long ceased to have any meaning at all in his blindfolded world—this might be tomorrow, or several tomorrows, after that hour when he had dumped the animals in the Wild.

The animals! Once more he put his newly alerted mind to trying to establish contact with them. If they had been located and captured, he could not tell, for to all his soundless calls there came no replies.

Click of boot soles, the scrape of the door panel, boot soles again much louder. Then the smell of clothes worn about animals too long—the odor of a human body. Troy found a snatch of time in which to marvel at his heightened sense of smell.

There was a tug at the bindings about his ankles, those bonds pulled off. Then a hand dug fingers into his shoulder.

"Up and walk, Dippleman! You go on your own two feet this time."

He staggered a step or two, brought up painfully against the sharp edge of a box. The hand came again to steer him with a shove that made him waver. So propelled, he emerged into the courtyard, heard the purr of a waiting flitter ready to take off.

His guard steered him to the flyer, and he was loaded by two men, not into the driver's seat but once more into that storage space in which he had ridden back to Tikil. He was sure of only two things: that Zul was in charge of his transportation—he had heard the small man's grunt of assent from the pilot's seat before they lifted—and that the Thieves' Guild, Blasterman's Section (highest paid of all the illegal services on Korwar), was in command of the prisoner's keeping, which was enough to dampen thoroughly all hopes of escape, or even of a try at defense.

Seventeen

But their lift into space was a very short one—perhaps it only cleared the division between courtyard and street. They descended gently, the wheels touched

195

pavement, and the flitter proceeded as a ground car. Which meant that their destination was somewhere within the business sector of the city and not one of the outlying villas. A warehouse—an office? It would have to be where the entrance of a blindfolded, bound man, accompanied by at least one guard, would not attract attention. If this was night, a goal in the business district or among the warehouses would meet those requirements.

Troy tried to remember the geography of Tikil in relation to Kyger's but found that a hopeless task. Unless he was on his feet in the open, his eyes unbandaged, he could not even effectively retrace his way to the Dipple.

They turned once, twice, their speed a decourous one well within the limit. And undoubtedly they were taking every precaution against any irregularity of action or appearance that could awaken suspicion in a patroller's mind. The Guild were skilled workmen and this was a Guild protection project, which meant that Troy might well be on his way to some hidden headquarters of that power. Only he did not believe so. It was more likely he was being taken to face, or at least be inspected by, Zul's new employer.

Another turn. Neither man in the driver's seat spoke. Troy deduced by the volume of street noise that the hour must be one of late evening. They had joined homeward-bound traffic, which meant they were *not* heading toward the warehouses.

The flitter came to a stop. Troy, with his heightened sense of smell and hearing, knew that one of the men had leaned across the partition and was hanging head and shoulders above him.

196

"Listen, you." The words were bitten off dryly, and Troy knew that the speaker meant them. "You are going to get out and walk, Dippleman. And you are going to do it nice and easy without any noise or confusion. I'll have a nerve-block grip on you all the way. Make any trouble and you will still walk—but not nice and easy. You will sweat blood with every step. Understand?"

Troy nodded his head violently, hoping that the other could see that gesture. He had not the slightest desire to suffer the promised correction for the fault of causing his captor any trouble.

The other assisted him out of the flitter and kept a tight fingerhold on him. They walked, as his guard had promised, "nice and easy" across a strip of pavement.

Troy sniffed vegetation. They must be in a dwelling-house district. There was a slight pause, probably waiting for the householder to release a door-panel lock. Then their slow march started once again, the click of boot heels deadened by foam-set floor covering.

Troy's head jerked suddenly. Just as he had known they had returned him to Kyger's storeroom, so did he now guess where he stood. There could not be two such establishments in Tikil! But knowledge brought with it complete bewilderment—almost shock.

What did the clerk Dragur, living in the midst of a collection of marine horrors, have to do with Kyger's secret employment?

On the other hand—Troy's thoughts readjusted quickly—the colorless man's chosen hobby was an excellent cover for a connection between him and the shop, a connection above suspicion, since Dragur's enthusiasm concerning his pet monsters in their globes

197

and aquariums had not been feigned; Troy would swear to that. His only objection to this new revelation was the character of the man himself. He simply could not visualize Dragur as the mastermind behind anything but fussy details of Korwarian bureaucracy.

Troy's ears caught the faint plop-plop of water slapping in a bowl as some inhabitant of the marine zoo moved, and he tried to remember how the room had been laid out at the time of his first visit there.

"Here is your man, Citizen, safe and in one piece." That was his guard reporting.

"Most commendable," Dragur's slightly high-pitched voice replied. "But I understand that the shipment is not complete. We were to have a complete shipment, Guildsman, complete."

"You shall have to ask this one what he did with the others, Citizen. The Big Man will settle with you on the deal. Give me the delivery release."

"Your Big Man shall also make an adjustment on the fee," Dragur snapped. "I bargained for a complete shipment. No release until that matter is settled."

"The Big Man will not feel kindly about that, Citizen." This was no threat, just a statement of fact, a fact to be accepted when the Guild made it clear.

"Oh, he will not? Well, I share his disappointment!" Dragur actually giggled. "You may tell him that as soon as you wish."

"No release, no delivery." The grip on Troy tightened.

"And you think you may march out of here, taking him with you?"

There was a long moment of silence. Troy tried to imagine what might be happening that he could not see.

198

"Where did you get that?" his guard asked slowly.

"I do not ask questions about the source of *your* equipment, do I?" countered Dragur. "Now you will remove your hands from my shipment and you will withdraw to your flitter. You have my permission, however, to communicate with your Big Man if you wish. I do not know whether he suffers bungling with patience or not. His reaction to your report you are better able to gauge than I. But you may mention to him, as a mitigating point, that a profitable relationship between ourselves may not be at an end, providing, of course, that we come to an equitable agreement now. I will also indicate that I have contracted for a time guardianship with your organization and that still has several hours to run. I am not in any way breaking contract."

The hand fell away from Troy. With the grunt of a baffled man who had been outmaneuvered, the guard moved from his side, and a moment later a door panel opened and closed. Troy heard Dragur laugh again.

"He will beam in his Big Man as soon as he thinks matters over. Better get a rating now than a burn later for not reporting."

"The Guildsmen like their credits." Zul spoke for the first time.

"But of course, do not all of us? On the other hand their continuing in business—at least the continuance of this particular branch of their business—depends also on a certain integrity. If they promise a shipment in full and deliver only part, then they have broken contract and must take the consequences. But that is a matter to be taken under advisement later. Now, Zul, let us make our visitor more comfortable."

Fingers pulled at the cords about Troy's wrists. His arms fell to his sides and then he rubbed his hands together. Another tug and the blindfold was a loop about his throat. He was blinking, dazzled by the light, subdued as it was, in the room.

"A most energetic young man—"

Troy centered his attention on the speaker. Dragur sat there in a most unusual chair. A tall glass slab formed the back, and in it swam with oily ease one of the miniature nightmare monsters, coming to the fore now and then as if peering over its master's shoulder, or to whisper through the transparent pane into his ear. Similar aquariums on either side, one holding carnivorous dorch crabs and the other a tramjan reef snake, served as armrests. The lid of the crab container was up, and from time to time Dragur tossed in small wriggling creatures to satisfy his pets' hunger. As an arrangement designed to make the onlooker both queasy and disinclined to argue with its owner, it was extremely successful.

But across Dragur's sharp-boned knees there also rested a nerve needler. And, seeing that, Troy could well understand the quick and almost fearful withdrawal of the Guildsman.

"You must be tired," Dragur continued in his high, fussy voice. "So much traveling and most of it under what might be termed uncomfortable conditions. Zul, provide Horan with a seat. There is no need for you to be uncomfortable here. No—I believe in comfort. Ehh—that is it, my pretty! Jump!" He was dangling a tidbit over the crab cage. "Did you note that, my boy? Such energy, such spirit! One could not believe that a crab could actually leap, now, could one? I have discovered

200

that many things will cause a crab, or an animal, or a man, to exert himself far past the powers one believes that nature endows him with at birth. Many things—"

"Such as a needler?"

Zul had brought a chair, not one furnished with attendant monster cages, Troy was pleased to note, and he sat down.

"A most crude stimulant to endeavor, only to be used in special cases and under special conditions. No, the action obtained under threat of punishment or death cannot be depended upon for any length of time. Just as torture is an expedient to be tried only by the unimaginative. A man will admit anything to save himself from pain when his breaking point has been found. Needlers have their places. I prefer more attractive methods."

"Such as?" Troy tried not to watch a second exhibition of profitable greed in the crab cage.

"Such as—" But whatever Dragur was about to say was silenced by a low buzz.

Zul, blaster in hand, sped across the room and vanished through an inner door. Dragur raised the needler so that the spray barrel sighted on Troy.

"Perhaps I am wrong," he said in a voice that was this time neither high nor fussy. "This may be an occasion for the cruder settlement after all. Sit where you are, Horan. The slightest move will compel me to press the trigger on this, and I think you know the results of such an action. I will also be compelled to do the same at any vocal warning from your direction. If we do have an unfriendly visitor on the way, he will encounter some surprises." With his other hand Dragur snapped down the lid of the crab cage, and in the quiet only the noises of the aquarium dwellers could be heard.

Then there was the sound of a scuffle, followed by a thud. Dragur, Troy noted, did not turn his head in that direction; his full attention was still fixed on his prisoner.

"An intruder indeed." The agent's voice was now hardly more than a whisper. "And I believe that he has fallen into one of our amusing little traps. We shall soon know."

They did. Zul led the small procession. Behind him stumbled a man who wove about on rubbery legs, the normal gait of one who has taken a half jolt from a stunner in the motor nerves. And holding him erect and on course was the same Guildsman who had explored the flitter when Troy had been a captive to the pinner beam in the Wild. But it was the identity of the prisoner that startled Troy. Rerne!

Just as he had not expected to find the ranger in his trap in the cavern of the Ruhkarv, so he had not foreseen his arrival not only in Tikil but in this particular house.

Dragur surveyed the new captive.

"Greetings to the noble Hunter." He used the exaggerated phrase demanded by formal society with a sardonic inflection. "Not that I quite understand why one of the Clans should be moved to enter my modest home by the rear entrance and that without invitation from me. Zul, a chair for our new guest, please. We are becoming quite crowded here, are we not? So you—" He watched the Guildsman slide Rerne onto the seat of the chair Zul drew forward. "You might as well retire, guard. Be sure I shall inform your Big

Man of your alert and most appreciated services. I trust, Hunter Rerne," he said to the new captive, "your head is sufficiently clear for you to note and be duly apprehensive of this importation of mine." The needler lifted a fraction of an inch and then went back into a new position, one that would share its deadly and agonizing spray between his prisoners.

"These interruptions quite put one off." Dragur shook his head. "We were in the midst of a most serious conversation, Hunter."

"Then I ask pardon for the disturbance." Again the formal words. Save for his loss of control over his muscles, it would appear that Rerne had not been stun-beamed to the point where he suffered too much.

"Most gracious of you, noble Hunter. Time presses or we could resume our conference later and in more privacy, Horan. But you have no ties with the Clans. Or have you? This sudden and unheralded arrival of the noble Hunter is provocative."

His head slightly atilt, Dragur looked speculatively from Troy to Rerne and back again.

The ranger turned a countenance of blank courtesy to his captor as he replied, "Your men left a trail that was easy enough to follow, Citizen. When a trace of that sort leads from the Wild to Tikil, we are interested."

"Interested!" Dragur repeated that word as if he would wring more than one fine shade of meaning from it. His attention returned to Troy, and the latter had his own reply ready. He did not know why Rerne had followed him here, but he was not going to be drawn into any business of the Clans.

"I have no ties with the Wild." And the emphasis

he put on the statement made it sound unduly harsh in that crowded room.

"And I shall accept that assurance, Horan. It is easy to believe that you do not have much sympathy for any authority on Korwar."

"And I am not a Guildsman."

"Have I suggested such a thing?" Dragur demanded. "I merely comment upon certain unpleasant facts of life. You surely cannot nurse any fondness for the Dipple, nor accordingly for the laws that have confined you there. On the other hand"—his fingers moved to one of the seam pockets of his tunic, came out to display a white card—"this is your permission to leave this world."

"Going where?"

"Norden."

The answer was so unexpected that Troy was as shocked as if he had met a needler face on. Then caution, learned painfully through the years, took cool control of his brain again. He hoped he had given no outward sign of his shock and surprise, knowing that Dragur was perhaps the most dangerous man he had ever faced—not because of the outlawed off-world weapon he now held across his knees, but because he did not really have to use it. The agent was right, there were other ways to bend a man to his will, and he had just produced an effective one to level Troy Horan.

"Why?" Troy came out with the question flatly.

"Let us say that I have—"

"A tidbit for a crab to jump for?" Troy countered. He was afraid, afraid with a different sort of chill than that which had seeped along his backbone when he had faced the needler.

"A tidbit, just so. Norden is now under the jurisdiction of the Confederation. The Horan holding there was, I believe, the Valley of the Forest Range—a good-sized range—a very fruitful one. There was the stockade of the Home Place, and five out-towers, a fruit setting, and an excellent stand of skin-wood in the heights. Quite a pleasant little kingdom of your own, Range Master Horan, was it not? Your family and their riders must have been practically self-sufficient. Such a pity—less than a century to grow and all swept away by the arbitrary orders of one man with his mind on a war that did not even come near that planet. Commander Di was impulsive, a little too firm a believer in his own edicts.

"I fear you will have to do some reorganizing and start from the beginning along some lines. The tupan have run wild. But a roundup should bring them under brand control again. And you will be permitted to recruit your own riders, as well as be given all possible assitance from Confederation officers."

"Promising quite a lot, are you not, Citizen?" Troy kept as tight a control over his emotions as he could. Every one of Dragur's words had been a whip laid on sensitive skin. He dared not believe that there was a fraction of truth in the offer, dared not for the sake of his own equilibrium of heart and mind.

"I am promising nothing that I cannot deliver, Range Master Horan." And in that moment Troy was forced to believe him.

"Korwar is a Council planet." Troy hedged, tried to test his assurance from another angle.

"Which again means nothing—to me." And once more his tone and the will behind it carried conviction.

"And in return for Norden what do you ask?"

"A small task successfully performed—by you, Range Master. It seems by some quirk of fate you alone now on this world are able to communicate with some runaway servants of mine. I want them back, and you can get them for me."

That was it: produce the animals—and get Norden. Norden and everything his father had held ten years ago! Simple and deadly as that.

"They must be very special, these servants of yours," Rerne cut in.

"Indeed, noble Hunter, as you already know. Their breeding is the result of many years of research and experimentation. They are the only ones of their species—"

"On Korwar." Rerne's words were not a question, but a statement that carried both force and meaning. Troy caught the inference. Yes, the five he had left in the Wild might be the only ones of their species on Korwar. And yet in other places, other solar systems, similar tools were being employed by Confederation agents.

Dragur shifted slightly in the weird chair. "What happens on other planets is none of my concern, noble Hunter, nor the Clans'. In fact I will assure you that once my servants are returned to me, there shall be no cause to fear any more activity of this type on
206

Korwar. The experiment, due to the human element here, has been a failure. We shall admit defeat and withdraw."

And that, too, Troy believed.

"And the animals themselves?"

"Are now expendable. I do not think that you will hesitate for a moment to weigh the lives of five animals against your return to Norden, will you, Range Master?"

Troy's tongue tip wet his dry lips. He had to use all his will power to fight shivers running along arms and legs.

"You cannot be sure I can bring them in."

"No, but you are the only contact with them. And I think my crab will jump with all his energy for this tidbit, do you not agree?"

"Yes!" Troy's answer came in a harsh explosion of breath. "Yes, I do!" He saw, from the corner of his eye, Rerne's head turn in his direction, a flash of surprise deepen to bleak distaste on the ranger's face. But Rerne's opinion of him could not matter now. He must keep thinking of the future. Dragur was so right; this crab was willing to jump—very high!

"So!" The agent spoke to Rerne now. "You see how simply matters can be arranged. There is no need for Clan interference—or their hope to have a hand in this. I take it, Range Master, that the animals still *are* in the Wild?"

"They left the flitter for the woods just before your men slapped that pinner on me."

"How easy to understand once one knows the facts. Very well, we need have no worries now. You, noble

Hunter, shall be our passport to the Wild. A happy chance brought you here in time. One might almost begin to believe in the ancient superstitions regarding a personified form of Fate that could favor or strike adversely at a man. We shall be a hunting party, just Zul and I, you, noble Hunter, Range Master Horan, and my Guildsman. And if all goes well, we shall have this matter decided before nightfall tomorrow. I am sure we are all sensible men here and there will be no trouble." He raised the needler.

Troy was not sure Rerne noted that warning gesture. When the ranger replied, his voice was remote.

"There is no argument, Citizen. I am at your service."

"But, of course, noble Hunter, did I not say you would be? And now we shall go."

Eighteen

Troy had no idea how far into the Wild they had penetrated. As Dragur had foreseen, Rerne talked them safely through the Clan patrols. Dawn came and mellowed into day, the day sped west as they bore east. Troy put his head back against the cabin walls, closed his eyes, but not to sleep.

His right hand braceleted his left wrist, moving around and around on the smooth, cool surface of the band he had involuntarily worn out of Ruhkarv, until that movement fell into rhythm with his reaching thoughts.

The flitter moved at top speed, but surely thought could thrust farther and faster than any machine. He tried to call up a sharp picture of that tongue of woodland into which the animals had fled—was it hours, or days ago? Simba, if he could contact Simba! If he could persuade the cat, and through him the others, to come back to that meeting point, be waiting there—

Norden— No, he must not think of Norden now, of how it would be to ride free once more down the valley. With a wrench of thought that was close to physical pain, Troy crushed down memory and dreams born of that memory. He must concentrate with every part of him, mental and physical, on the job at hand.

There was only Dragur's word that none of them here could communicate with the animals. But if that was not true, why did they want his help so badly?

His whole body was taut with effort. He was not aware that his face grew gaunt with strain or that dark finger-shaped bruises appeared under his eyes. He did not know that Rerne was watching him again with an intentness that approached his own concentration.

Slip, slip, right, left, his fingers on the bracelet—his silent call fanning out ahead of the ship. Troy aroused to chew a concentrate block passed to him, hardly conscious of the others in that cabin, so tired only his will flogged him into that fruitless searching.

And to undermine his labors there was a growing dismay. Perhaps the animals, having witnessed his capture, had pressed on past any hope of their being located now. Only Sahiba's injury could curtail such a flight.

Nightfall found the flitter well into the plains. Dragur heeded the protests of the Guildsman who alternated with Zul as pilot and agreed to camp for the night.

"Which," the agent remarked with courtesy exaggerated enough to approach a taunt, "provides us with a problem, noble Hunter. You, in this, your home territory, will have to be bodily restrained. I trust you will forgive the practical solution. Our young friend here needs no such limits on his freedom."

Rerne, hands and feet bound, made no protest as he was bedded down between Zul and the Guildsman. Troy, oblivious to his company and surroundings, fell asleep almost at once, his weariness like a vast weight grinding him into darkness. Yet in that dark there was no rest. He twisted, turned, raced breathlessly to finish some fantastic task under the spur of time. And he awoke gasping, sweat damp upon his body.

Stars were paling overhead. This was the dawn of the day in which they would come to the wood. For a fraction of one fast escaping moment he knew again that sensation of freedom and fresh life that had first come to him on the plateau, which would always signify for him the Wild. Then that was gone under the lash of memory. Troy did not stir, save that his hand unconsciously once more sought the band on his wrist, and from the touch of that strange metal a quickening of spirit reached into body and mind. His thoughts quested feverishly, picturing the fringe of saplings and trees as he had seen it last. Simba crouched beneath a bush—waiting—

"Found!"

Troy flung up his arm, the cool band of Ruhkarv pressed tight to his forehead above his closed eyes. And under that touch his mental picture leaped into instant sharp detail.

"You come?"

"I come," Troy affirmed silently. "Be ready—when I come." He tried to marshal the necessary arguments and promises that would draw them to the place where Dragur would land.

"So—you have made contact at last, Range Master?"

Troy's arm fell away from his forehead. He frowned up at the Confederation agent. But there was no reason to deny the truth. What he had had to do he had done, to the best of his ability.

"Yes. They will be waiting."

"Excellent. I must compliment you, Horan, on your commendable speed in seeking to fulfill your part of the bargain. We shall eat and then get on to the netting."

Troy ate slowly. So much depended now on Simba's response to his appeal, on the cat's dominance over his fellow mutants. If the slight bond between man and animals was not stout enough to lead them to trust him now—then he had failed completely.

Back in the flitter he made no further attempt to keep in touch with the fugitives. He had done all he could during that early morning contact. Either they would be waiting—or they would not. The future must be governed by one or the other of those facts—which one he would not know until the flyer landed.

In midmorning, bright and clear, the flitter touched with an expert's jarless landing at the edge of the wood. Dragur ordered them out, the barrel of his needler as much on Troy as on Rerne.

"And now"—the agent faced the woodland—"where are they, Horan?"

"In there." Troy nodded to the cover. Yes, they were all there, waiting in hiding. Whether they would show themselves was again another matter.

The Guildsman drew his blaster, thumbed the butt dial to spray beam. Troy gathered himself for a quick leap if the other touched the button. But the agent spoke first. "No beaming," he snapped. "We have to be sure we get them all and in one attack." Then he turned to Troy. "Bring them out."

"I have no summoner, and they will not obey me to that point. I cannot bring them against their wills. I can only hold them where they are."

For a second or two he was afraid that Dragur would refuse to enter the shadow of the trees. Then Troy's statement apparently made sense to the agent.

"March!" Dragur's tone sheared away the urbanity of earlier hours. Troy obeyed, the agent close behind him, needler ready.

Horan rounded a bush, stooped under a hanging branch. "Here! Here! Here!"

Simba, Sargon, Sheba—

Troy threw himself face down into the leaf mold, rolled—Dragur shrieked. Troy came to his knees again and faced the man now plunging empty-handed toward him.

Simba clung with three taloned feet to the agent's shoulder, as with a fourth he clawed viciously at the man's face and eyes, while both foxes made a concen-
212

trated attack with sharp fangs upon the agent's ankles.

Troy caught up the needler the other had dropped when Simba had sprung to his present perch from a low-hanging tree limb. Horan was still on one knee, but he had the weapon up to cover Zul as the small man burst through the bushes to them.

"Stand—and drop that!"

Zul's eyes widened. Reluctantly his fingers loosened their hold upon the blaster. The weapon thudded to the ground.

"You, too!"

The Guildsman who had prodded Rerne on into this pocket clearing obeyed Troy's order. A furred shadow with a long tail crooked above its back flitted out of cover, mouthed Zul's blaster and brought it to Troy, then went back for the guard's weapon. Dragur staggered around, his arms flailing about his head where the blood dripped from ripped flesh on his face and neck. Simba no longer rode his shoulders, but was now assisting the foxes to drive the man, with sudden rushes and slashes at his feet and legs.

Blinded, crying in pain, completely demoralized by the surprise and the unexpected nature of that attack, the agent tripped and fell, sprawling at Rerne's feet, while Simba snarled and made a last claw swipe at his face. The ranger stared in complete amazement from the team of animal warriors to Troy.

"You planned this?" he asked in a voice loud enough to carry over Dragur's moaning.

"*We* planned this," Troy corrected. He thrust the

213

two blasters into his belt, but he kept the needler aimed at the others.

"Now"—he motioned to the Guildsman—"you gather up Citizen Dragur and we will go back to the flitter."

There was no argument against the needler. Half carrying the moaning agent, the Guildsman tramped sullenly back to the flyer, Zul and Rerne in his wake, Troy bringing up the rear. He knew the animals were active as flanking scouts though he no longer saw them.

"You"—Troy nodded to Rerne—"unload water, the emergency supplies."

"You are staying here then?" The ranger showed no surprise.

"*We* are staying," Troy corrected once again, watching as the other dumped from the flitter the things he might need for survival in the Wild. Then the Guildsman, under Horan's orders, gave Dragur rough first aid, tied him up and stowed him away, afterwards doing the same for Zul, before he, himself, submitted to binding at Rerne's hands.

"And how do you pr ose to deal with me?" the ranger asked as he boosted the last of the invaders from Tikil into the flitter.

"You can go—with them." Troy hesitated for a moment and then, almost against his will, he added roughly, "I ask your pardon for that tap on the head at Ruhkarv."

Rerne gazed at him levelly. The mask he had worn in the city was back, to make his features unreadable, though there was a spark of some emotion deep in his eyes.

"You were within your rights—an oath breaker deserves little consideration." But behind those flat words was something Troy thought he could read a different meaning into.

"Those waiting were not your men but patrollers?" He demanded confirmation of what he had come to suspect.

Simba appeared out of the grass, by his presence urging an end to this time-wasting talk.

"So you saw that much." The flicker in Rerne's eyes glowed stronger.

"I saw, and I have had time to think." It was an apology, one Troy longed for the other to accept, though that acceptance could lead to nothing between them now save a level balancing of the old scales.

"I will come back—you understand that?" Rerne stated a fact.

Troy smiled. The headiness of his victory bubbled in him. Release from the strain of the past hours, or past days, was an intoxicant he found hard to combat.

"If you wish, Rerne. I may not be your equal in the lore of the Wild, but together we shall give you a good run—"

"We?" Rerne's head swung. If he was looking for the other animals, he would not see them. But they were all there, even to Sahiba crouched under the low branches of a bush.

"Still *we*."

"And Norden?"

Troy's smile faded. That was a wicked backstroke he had not expected from Rerne. His braceleted hand went to the belt where the studs were no longer burnished bright.

"The crab did not jump," he replied evenly.

"Perhaps it was not offered the right bait." Rerne shook his head. "This is the Wild and you are no trained ranger. By our laws I cannot help you unless you ask for it, and that would mean surrender." He waited a long moment, as if he actually hoped for some affirmative sign from Troy.

The other nodded. "I know. From now on it will be you and yours against us. Only do not be too sure of the ending, Rerne."

He watched the flitter rise in the vertical climb of a master pilot. Then the carrying strap of the needler across his shoulder, he made a compact bundle of the supplies.

Sunset, sunrise, another nightfall—morning again—though here the sun made a pale greenish shimmer in the forest depths. Troy only knew that they were still pointed east. At least under such cover he could not be tracked by air patrols. Those hunting him would have to go afoot and so be subject to discovery by the keener senses of the animals. Shang took to the treetops, Simba and the foxes ranged wide on the ground, able to scout about Troy as he marched, carrying Sahiba.

Once Simba had been stalked in turn by a forest creature, and Troy had blasted it into a charred mass as it leaped for the cat. But otherwise they saw few living things as they pushed forward.

To Troy the Wild did not threaten. About him it closed like a vast envelope of content. And the memory of Norden was a whisper of mist torn away by the wind rustling through the boughs over his head. With the animals he had moved into a new world, and Tikil too was a forgotten dream—a nightmare—small, far-off, cramped and dusty, well lost. The only thing to
216

trouble him was a vague longing now and then for one of his own kind to share the jubilation of some discovery, the exultation when he awoke here feeling a measure of his birthright returned to him.

On the fifth day the ground began to rise, and once or twice through a break in the trees Troy located peaks in the sky ahead. Perhaps in those heights he could find a cave to shelter them—something they would need soon if the now threatening clouds meant a storm.

"Men!"

Troy froze. The sobering shock made him recoil against a tree. He had half forgotten the chase behind. Now he heard Simba squall in fear and rage, the fear thrusting into Troy's brain in turn as a spearhead. A pinner! The same force that had gripped him at the time of Zul's pursuit glued them all to the earth once again. Yet there was no flitter in sight, no sign of a tracker.

"How far away?" he appealed to the scouts.

"Up slope—they are coming closer now." From three sides he had his replies as noses caught scents he could not detect. "They have set a trap."

Troy tried to subdue the rising panic of the animals. Yes, a good trap. But how had they known that Troy and his companions would emerge from the wood at that point? Or had they laid down a long barrier of pinner beams just in case?

There was no chance for him to use the needler; he could not raise his hand to the blasters at his belt. All of them would remain where they were to await the leisure of the unseen enemy. And the bitterness of that soured in his mouth, cramped his now useless muscles.

Sahiba whimpered in his hold. The others were quiet now, understanding his trap explanation. He knew that each small mind was busy with the problem—one that they could not solve. Not singly—but together?

Why had he thought that? Swiftly Troy touched each mind in turn—Simba, Sargon, Sheba, Shang, Sahiba. Simba must be their choice for the experiment. The black cat whose whole battle technique depended upon quiet stalking, instant, lightning-swift attack. If they could free Simba—!

This was a last fantastic attempt, but the only one left to them. Troy focused the full force of his mind on a picture of Simba free, Simba moving one padded paw skillfully before the other as he crept up the slope before them to locate the pinner broadcaster. The others took up that picture, fed into it their combined will and mind force. The thread became a beam, a beam of such strength as to amaze one part of Troy's brain, even as he labored to build it deeper, wider, tougher.

A trickle of moisture zigzagged down his cheek. It was crazy to hope that mind could triumph over a body pinned. Perhaps only because of the freedom of the past few days could their desperate need nourish such a hope. Troy was weak, drained. Yet, as he had fought to reach the animals from the flitter, so now he labored to unleash Simba. And in that moment he knew that it could be done!

Troy did not see that small streak of black bounding up the hillside. And the man operating the pinner could not have seen it coming. There was a howl of pain from above, and Troy was free. He leaped out of the brush and went to one knee, the needler ready to sweep the whole territory ahead.

Rerne arose from behind a rock well up the slope, his hands up and empty. Out of the grass sped Sargon, Sheba, Shang, and, descending in a series of bounds, Simba. Once more Troy was one in their half circle of defense and offense.

"You broke pinner power!" Rerne came down at an even pace, his eyes never leaving Troy's face.

"And you found us." In spite of his overwhelming victory against the machine, Troy tasted the ultimate defeat. The Wild no longer remained their coveted escape.

"We found you." Rerne jerked one hand in a signal. Two more men started to move along the hillside, their hands conspicuously up and empty. One was Rogarkil; the other wore the uniform of a Council attaché.

Rerne spoke to them over his shoulder. "So—now have you seen for yourselves?"

"You underestimated the danger!" The Council attaché's voice was harsh and rough, he was breathing fast through his nose, and it was plain he did not find his present position one that he relished.

"Danger," Rerne observed, "is relative. Belt knives have been shifted from the sheath of one wearer to that of another without losing their cutting edge. You might consider the facts in this case before you commit those you represent to any hasty course of action."

Clansman spoke to Council as an equal, and, though the attaché did not like it, here in the Wild he must accept that. His mouth was now a tight slit of disapproval. In another place and company those lips would be shaping orders to make men jump.

"I protest your arguments, Hunter!"

Rogarkil answered in a mild tone. "Your privilege, Gentle Homo. Rerne does not ask that you agree; he merely requires that you report, and that the matter be taken under sober consideration. I will say also that one does not throw away a new thing merely because it is strange—until one explores its usefulness. This is the Wild."

"And you rule here? The Council shall remember that also!"

Rogarkil shrugged. "That is also your privilege."

With a last glare at Troy and the animals, the officer strode back up the hill, joined, when he was at the crest, by an escort of patrollers who gathered in from the rocks. Then he was gone, as the wind brought the first gust of the storm down upon them all.

"Truce?" asked Rerne, his shoulders hunched against the elements. Then he smiled a little.

Troy hesitated only for a moment before his own hand went up in answer and he slung the needler. He ran toward the shelter the ranger had indicated, a space between two leaning rocks. The area so sheltered was small, and they were still two companies, Troy and the animals on one side, the Clansmen on the other.

"That one will do some straighter thinking on the way back to Tikil," Rerne remarked.

Rogarkil nodded. "Time to think is often enough. When and if they do move, we shall be ready."

"Why are you doing this?" Troy demanded, guessing from the crosscurrents of their speech that, incredibly, the Clans seemed to be choosing his side.

"Because," Rerne replied, "we do believe what I said just now to Hawthol—a knife changing sheaths remains a knife. And it can be used even to counter a blow

220

from its first owner. Kyger died because of a personal feud. But for that chance this attack against the Council, and against Korwar, would have succeeded. And because this espionage conspiracy was in a manner aimed against Korwar, it concerns us. Our guests here, the Great Ones of the galaxy, must be protected. As we told you that night in Tikil, the continuance of our way of life here depends in turn upon their comfort and safety. Anything that undermines that is a threat to the Clans.

"Now if the Confederation tries this weapon on another planet, well, that is the Council's affair. But such an attack is finished here. And I do not believe that Kyger, or Dragur, or any of those behind them ever realized or cared about the other potentials of the tools they developed to further their plan. It could be very illuminating to see what might happen when two or three species long associated in one fashion move into equality with each other, to work as companions, not as servants and masters—"

"And who is better fitted to make such a study than the Clans?" asked Rogarkil.

Troy stiffened. They were taking too much for granted. Both men and animals must have some voice in their future.

"Will the crab jump to his bait, Horan?" Rerne leaned forward a little, raising his voice above the gathering fury of the storm. "Rangers' rights in the Wild for you and your company here—granting us in return the right to know them better? This may not rank with being a Range Master on Norden—"

He paused nearly in mid-word at Troy's involuntary wince. But that hurt was fading fast. Troy's thought

221

touched circle with the other five. He did not urge, tried in no way to influence them. This was their decision more than his. And if they did not wish to accept—well, he still had the needler.

The answer came. Troy raised his chin, looked to the rangers with a cool measurement such as he could not have used a week earlier, but which was now part of him.

"If you make that a trial agreement—"

Rerne smiled. "Caution is good in a man—and his friends. Very well, rangers, this shall be a trial run as long as you wish it so. I will admit that I am eager to have a catseye view of life—if you will allow me into this hitherto closed company of yours."

Troy's eyes met Rerne's and the younger man drew an uneven breath. Norden's plains were gone now. Instead he had a flash of another memory. A rock-walled room on a cliff above a lake and Rerne's voice talking of this world and its fascinating concerns.

"Why?" He did not stop to think that perhaps his question, which seemed so clear to him, might not be as intelligible to the other. But—as if Rerne's thought could touch his like the animals'—the other answered him: "We are of one kind, plains rider." Then Rerne looked beyone the man to the animals. "So shall we all be in the end."

"So be it." Troy agreed, knowing now he spoke the truth.

GREAT ROMANTIC NOVELS

SISTERS AND STRANGERS   PB 04445 $2.50
by Helen Van Slyke

Three women—three sisters each grown into an independent lifestyle—now are three strangers who reunite to find that their intimate feelings and perilous fates are entwined.

THE SUMMER OF THE SPANISH WOMAN
                                CB 23809 $2.50
by Catherine Gaskin

A young, fervent Irish beauty is alone. The only man she ever loved is lost as is the ancient family estate. She flees to Spain. There she unexpectedly discovers the simmering secrets of her wretched past . . . meets the Spanish Woman . . . and plots revenge.

THE CURSE OF THE KINGS   CB 23284 $1.95
by Victoria Holt

This is Victoria Holt's most exotic novel! It is a story of romance when Judith marries Tybalt, the young archeologist, and they set out to explore the Pharaohs' tombs on their honeymoon. But the tombs are cursed . . . two archeologists have already died mysteriously.

8000